Please return on or before the latest date above.
You can renew online at *www.kent.gov.uk/libs*
or by telephone 08458 247 200

1/09 LP
Af

Loveday, Chrissie
Cranham's Curios.

CUSTOMER SERVICE EXCELLENCE

Libraries & Archives

00884\DTP\RN\07.07   LIB 7

CRANHAMS' CURIOS

After her hectic London life, Rachel returns to her native Cornwall and her parents' Curio shop. Things are changing and she realises that she is needed. There is plenty to do and the local vet, Charlie is an added incentive to extend her stay . . . but he has a serious girlfriend. Can she make a new life in St Truan or will she miss the city life? Will she stay for just a week or is it a lifetime commitment?

CHRISSIE LOVEDAY

CRANHAMS' CURIOS

Complete and Unabridged

LINFORD
Leicester

First published in Great Britain in 2007

First Linford Edition
published 2008

British Library CIP Data

Loveday, Chrissie
    Cranhams' curios.—Large print ed.—
    Linford romance library
    1. Cornwall (England: County)—Fiction
    2. Love stories 3. Large type books
    I. Title
    823.9'2 [F]

    ISBN 978–1–84782–297–0

Published by
F. A. Thorpe (Publishing)
Anstey, Leicestershire

Set by Words & Graphics Ltd.
Anstey, Leicestershire
Printed and bound in Great Britain by
T. J. International Ltd., Padstow, Cornwall

A Breath Of Fresh Air!

Jack Cranham was arranging a display of glass and china jugs in the window of Cranhams' Curios.

'Our Rachel will be here later on,' his wife, Audrey, called out to him from the tiny kitchen at the back of the shop-cum-tearoom, 'and you know what she's like — she'll have been home for no more than five minutes before she'll want to re-organise everything, so it's hardly worth your while bothering with that display.'

Audrey was making the day's supply of scones. Serving cream teas was a new venture for the Cranhams — the idea being that, after tucking into the traditional Cornish fare, the tearoom customers might then be tempted to browse around the antique shop and, hopefully, part with more cash!

Part of the shop had needed to be

1

screened off to serve the simple food, but so far it had proved a reasonably worthwhile enterprise.

'How long's Rachel planning to stay for this time?' Jack called back to his wife.

'Oh, you know our daughter. Five minutes or five weeks. Depends how busy she is up in London.'

'She hasn't said much about her job lately, has she?' commented Jack, wandering into the kitchen.

'I think she's getting fed up with it. There now. All done.' Audrey put the tray of scones into the oven and wiped her hands. 'Do you think we'll be busy today?'

'It's difficult to say. There are a few tourists about but it's early in the season yet. Mind you, the weather feels like spring!'

The shopkeepers of St Truan relied upon the holiday trade to make a living. On fine days during spring and summer, tourists would come to look at the quaint buildings and buy local produce from the village shops for their beach picnics. Then, when the weather was bad, the souvenir and craft shops were kept busy as the holidaymakers sought shelter from the elements and the little cafés were full of visitors relaxing over teas and coffees.

'What time is Rachel due to arrive?'

'I've simply no idea. You know what she's like. You can't expect her to be pinned down by something as simple as time!'

But suddenly the door was flung open and Rachel was there, in front of them.

'Mum! Dad! Wonderful to see you!' She threw her arms around her parents and hugged them close. 'You're looking tired, Mum. I hope you haven't been overdoing it? Oh, it's so lovely to be here! Can I smell fresh scones? Goody. And coffee?'

'The scones have only just gone into the oven,' protested Audrey, laughing. She was thrilled to see her pretty daughter. 'You've lost weight,' she scolded. 'Not been feeding yourself properly, I'd guess.'

'Why else would I come home?'

Rachel breezed around the shop, poking and prodding at various items of stock and wrinkling her nose.

'We need a big clear out! Some of this stuff's been here since before I left home. That must be all of four years ago.'

Jack laughed. His daughter would never change. She was still as bright and bubbly as when she'd been a little girl. Was she really twenty-five? Already? Or was it twenty-six?

'So, how long do we have your company for this time? Half a day or might it be a little longer?' he asked.

'Oh, Dad. I've no idea. Does it matter?'

'Of course not, love. We're delighted to see you for however long you can spare,' said Audrey, reaching down to open the oven door.

'I think these scones are ready now. What do you think, Jack?'

'No use asking me, love.'

Rachel frowned. Her mother never asked such questions. Especially of her father!

'Are you all right, Mum?'

'Of course I am, darling. Now, are you ready for one of these? I'll just make us all some coffee and we'll sit and have a natter. Whatever time did you leave London? It's only half past ten now.'

'I drove through the night. Easiest with all the traffic on the roads. As for road works, well, honestly, I reckon someone's bought a job lot of traffic cones and spread them out all over the country.'

The three of them sat round one of the little shop tables and drank the excellent coffee.

Rachel closed her eyes in bliss as she tucked into a fresh scone topped with jam and cream.

'Why did I ever leave Cornwall? St Truan is just as wonderful as ever, and you certainly haven't lost your touch at

5

baking, Mum. I never got around to breakfast this morning and that just hit the spot. So, what's the gossip? Tell me everything.'

One or two customers came and went but the family were able to chat in between attending to them, with Rachel putting on a pinny and serving trays of coffee and scones as they were needed.

She thought how good it would be to stay on in St Truan for a while, if only to help her parents in the shop. Just lately, her frenetic life in London had been getting her down and she'd longed for the peace and relaxed air of Cornwall. She was also a little concerned about her mother. There was something not quite right about her.

She yawned as her journey and lack of sleep began to catch up with her.

Eventually, she took her mother's advice and went out to the little cottage tucked away at the back of the shop. The two buildings weren't actually attached, but were separated only by a very narrow passageway.

Rachel had parked her car in the driveway, close to her parents' van that was looking decidedly old and past it. She noticed several new scrapes that had appeared since her last visit home and there were some patches of rust that clearly needed attention. She hauled her bags from her boot and went into the house.

It was so lovely to be home. She dragged her luggage up the narrow staircase, thinking how steep it must be for her mother's arthritic knees to cope with nowadays. Then, halfway up the stairs, she suddenly stopped, realising that her parents must both be nearing retirement age.

Never! Her mum and dad had always run the shop, and she couldn't believe they would ever give it up, and anyway, realistically, she doubted if they could afford to retire. They had made a reasonable living from the business but nothing spectacular.

Rachel shivered. She didn't even want to think of them getting older.

There was a very necessary comfort in knowing that everything would be just the same whenever she came home.

'Hello, Binkie,' she said as she looked up to see her mother's elderly cat sitting at the top of the stairs.

Binkie rubbed against her legs, miaowed, then jumped up on to the window-sill to see if anything interesting was going on outside.

'You're looking a bit older, too, aren't you?' She tickled under the cat's chin and Binkie gave a contented purr in response. 'I'll see you later, puss. Right now I need some sleep.'

She flung herself down on the bed that had been hers since childhood and very quickly fell asleep.

★ ★ ★

'Are you all right, dear?' she heard a voice calling, some hours later, as she dragged herself from her dreams. She sat up and gradually realised where she was.

'Mum? Yes, I'm fine. I must have

gone out like a light.'

Rubbing the sleep from her eyes, she went downstairs and into the kitchen.

'I can't believe I've slept so long. Have you finished in the shop?'

'Dad's just clearing up. I thought I'd get the meal going. Only a cottage pie but I know you love it.'

'Great. What can I do?'

'Peel the carrots? And there's broccoli in the fridge.'

Rachel grinned and put her arms around her mother's ample waist.

'It's so good to be home, Mum. No ready meals from the supermarket. Fresh veggies instead of tinned or frozen stuff. I really ought to move back here permanently.'

Her mother stood still for a moment.

'You are joking, I take it?'

'Erm . . . why? Would it be so terrible if I did move back home to live?'

'Of course not, dear. But I . . . I thought you were so independent these days. Busy life in the big city and all that.'

'Life in the big city's not all it's cracked up to be. Now, where are the carrots?'

As they worked side by side, Rachel couldn't help noticing that her mother wasn't as sure with the large cook's knife as she used to be, but she shrugged off the feeling of concern, and once everything was cooking and under control, she sat down at the kitchen table to flick through the local paper.

'You haven't started the crossword yet today,' she said to her mother. 'That's not like you.'

'Haven't had a minute. But go on. Read out the clues.'

'Five letters. '*Pale face, tradition in Cornwall*'?'

'Too obvious. Pasty.'

'Very good. Next clue. Six letters . . . '

The door opened and her father came in.

'All done, thank heavens. Something smells good. What are my favourite girls doing?'

'Just starting the crossword.'

'Oh, good. Your mother will like that. She hasn't been able to do it for a while. Can't see the little squares any more.'

'Jack. Be quiet, please. Now, are we going to open a bottle of wine? Celebrate the return of the lost sheep?'

'Is there something wrong with your eyes, Mum? Do you need new glasses?'

'She thinks she's got a cataract,' Jack replied. 'But she's too stubborn to admit there's a problem.'

Audrey scowled at him. Clearly it was the subject of some disagreement between them.

'Oh, Mum. That can be fixed with a simple operation and it would make all the difference to you. Why won't you see about it?'

'Lots of reasons. How would your father manage on his own? That's just for starters. Besides, I don't want to get one of those awful diseases they give you in hospitals.'

'That's plain silly. And they don't

keep you in for long these days. I could easily look after Dad and help in the shop while you're recovering. My scones might not be as good as yours, but they're quite edible. They should be after all your years of training.'

'I'll think about it. But aren't you supposed to have a job you can't be away from?'

It wasn't like Audrey to be so irritable and snappy. She was clearly not her usual happy self.

Rachel hesitated before answering.

'As a matter of fact, I'm thinking of leaving my job. I've had enough of the rat race. It would be nice to be footloose and fancy free for a while.'

'Oh, Rachel,' her father said reproachfully. 'We thought you were so happy! And really making something of your life.'

'I was. I am. Oh, I don't know. I need a break and some good clean Cornish air in my system. Time to think. And you should take advantage of my being here and take it a bit easier yourself,

Mum. I can help Dad. We can have a real good clear out and buy some new stock. Get everything running properly instead of muddling along the way you always do.'

'Well, thank you very much!' protested Jack. 'I'll have you know that our muddling along has given you a good start in life, young lady. Your mother and I have always done our best for you.'

'Oh, Dad, I'm so sorry. I didn't mean to sound ungrateful or to put down all you've done for me. See? I told you I've been living in London for too long. Got used to speaking a bit too directly.'

'Maybe it is time you got away from there then,' he answered, slightly mollified. 'I don't like to hear you talking like that. Now — what was the next crossword clue?'

He took off his shoes and pulled on the comfy old slippers he liked to wear. They were getting very tatty but he'd put away the new leather ones that Rachel had bought him last Christmas and continued to slop around in his battered old pair.

'I think this pie's done,' Audrey announced. 'Set the table, will you, dear?'

It was unclear which 'dear' she meant, so Rachel jumped up to do it, trying to make amends for having been so unforgivably hurtful to the two people she loved most in the world. She must be tired and grumpy and clearly needed a change.

'I really do want to help out so that you can have a bit of a rest, Mum. While I'm home I could easily look after the shop for the two of you and you could have the odd day out somewhere together. And don't look so worried. I promise not to upset anything or to rearrange the stock without asking you first.'

She raised her glass to them both.

★　★　★

Two days later, Rachel was busy altering the window display and had already set out a box of clearance items. Things that had been at the back of the shelves were given a polish and brought forward.

'We should put a vase of spring flowers in the window. Something eyecatching. And I might drape some yellow fabric over that old table. It would give an impact to that lovely tea-set. And that dear little child's chair could go in the window as well,' she burbled on excitedly.

Her parents sighed. So much for their daughter leaving everything as it was and not rearranging any of the stock. But truly, they loved it when she came home. She was a breath of fresh air in the place and some of her criticisms were valid. They did need to smarten up the place before the holiday season got going.

'Do what you think is best, dear,' her mother said. She was squinting at a shopping list and rubbing her eyes in frustration. When she noticed her daughter looking at her anxiously, she abandoned the list and busied herself with other things.

'Mum, why won't you go to the doctor? You really need to get your eyes sorted.'

'I'm fine. Stop fussing. It's nothing.'

'Pardon my disbelief. If it was Dad, you'd be nagging him, morning, noon and night. Go tomorrow. I'll hold the fort here.'

'And let myself in for weeks and weeks of waiting and uncertainty? Then more weeks recovering? I can't cope with all of that. No. I'll manage just fine the way I am.'

Rachel gave a small sigh. It had always been the same. If anyone in the family needed health care, her mother would bully them into going to the doctor or dentist. But when the patient was herself, a battle royal ensued to get her to seek help. But it was clear she had a problem, and it would only get worse.

Rachel decided to go to the doctor's surgery herself, as soon as she had the chance, and ask if they had any leaflets explaining about cataracts and their treatment. That way, she would be armed with the facts when it came to persuading her mother to do something before it was too late.

Just then her father came into the shop looking worried.

'Audrey, have you seen Binkie's ears? She's obviously got an infection. I think she needs to see the vet.'

'Oh, dear. When am I going to fit that in?'

'I'll take her,' Rachel offered. 'Has Mr Williams retired yet?'

'Charlie Williams is back at home and is gradually taking over the practice from his father. Well, in reality, he probably already has. His dad just does the odd clinic nowadays.'

'Charlie? I didn't know he'd come back to live in Cornwall. Well, well. I'll definitely take Binkie. Be good to catch up with him again. We had a bit of a thing going when we were at school, but then he went off to university and I went to work in London. We sort of lost touch.'

'I'd forgotten the two of you were close when you were younger. Such a nice young man. He was a real tearaway at one time, though. Him and that crowd he used to hang around with.'

'Well, he's grown up now. Probably married with a bunch of kids and a four-wheel drive.'

'He's got a four-wheel drive all right but I don't think he's married. Reg Williams would have said something, I'm sure.'

Rachel saw her parents exchange glances and her mother definitely had a matchmaker's glint in her eye.

★ ★ ★

Rachel made an appointment at the vet's, and next morning she carried a disgruntled Binkie along the village street in her pet-carrier to the surgery. There were several other people waiting, and Binkie miaowed pitifully, as if she was being severely maltreated.

'Mrs Cranham? You can go in now,' the receptionist called at last.

Rachel grinned and went through to the surgery.

'Hello, Charlie. How are you?'

'Rachel! Good heavens. I was expecting your mum. Well, don't you look good!'

He leaned over the examination table and gave her a peck on the cheek.

'Home on holiday?'

'Sort of. But I'm thinking of staying around for a while.'

'Great! We'll need to get together to catch up. How many years is it since I last saw you?'

'I suppose it must be getting on for seven years since those heady days of our youth.'

'We had fun, didn't we?' he said. 'That summer before we went our separate ways? I always mean to keep in touch but it never happens, does it? I suppose you're all settled now?' He reached for her hand and examined the

19

ring finger. 'No rings? No boyfriend?'

'Absolutely not!' She was amazed to find herself blushing. 'I . . . er . . . I've brought Mum's cat, Binkie, to see you. Her ears look infected.'

She opened the pet carrier and the cat hissed and shot out a paw.

'Now then, Binkie — it's only me. Come on.'

Charlie's voice was gentle and coaxing and soon the angry cat quietened down and allowed the young vet to ease her out of the carrier.

'Out you come, old girl. Oh, dear — you've been scratching at your ears again, haven't you?'

'It's nothing serious, is it?' Rachel asked anxiously. 'Only Mum will be upset if anything happens to Binkie, especially just now.'

'Oh? Why especially just now? Something wrong? I thought I hadn't seen your mum around for a while. She's OK, isn't she?'

'Yes, of course. Well, not really. Her eyesight's failing. We reckon she's got a cataract and she won't even get it looked at. Do you know anything about them? I need to get some information to convince her it's essential to have it fixed.'

'It's certainly a good idea to sort it sooner rather than later. It's a minor procedure and she could be out the same day. Excellent results and she should be able to see again in a day or two. Now, as for our feline friend, she needs a shot of antibiotics and I'll give you some cream. It's nothing serious.'

'Thanks. You're very good with her. I thought we were about to have problems just getting her out of the carrier.'

'It's all my years of training.'

'You always were a softie where animals were concerned. Collecting stray creatures and taking them home. You must have driven your parents crazy.'

'I'm sure I would have done but, don't forget, Dad's a vet, so taking home needy animals runs in the family.

Look, I'd really like to catch up with you properly, Rachel, but I have a string of patients to see just now. How about a drink this evening?'

'Yes, I'd like that.'

'I'll pick you up at seven-thirty?'

'That would be fine. Thanks, Charlie. It's really nice to see you again.'

She paid the bill at the desk and left the surgery.

Charlie had certainly grown into a very handsome man. He'd always been good looking at school, but now his features had firmed and his once blond hair had darkened, almost to a chestnut brown. His eyes were still the same startling blue and, against his tan, seemed to light his whole face.

She was looking forward to having a drink with him that evening, and smiled as she walked back to her parents' shop.

Rachel Settles In

'So, how did it go with Charlie?' her mother wanted to know as soon as Rachel got back from the vet's.

'Fine. It's just a slight infection. She's had an antibiotic jab and there's some cream.'

'And?'

'And what?' Rachel asked innocently.

'And is Charlie still the same as you remembered?'

'Not at all. He's all grown up.'

Her mother sighed in exasperation.

'You know what I mean.'

'He's still lovely, Mum, if that's what you mean. And we're going out together for a drink this evening.'

She was rewarded with a delighted grin from her mother.

'Now don't go getting ideas, Mum! It's just a drink to catch up, OK?'

'Of course it is, dear. Now, if you're

going out this evening that means an early supper. I'll pop back to the house at some point and get it going. You can stay in the shop and cover for me while I do that, can't you?'

'Yes, but don't worry about feeding me. I'm happy with a sandwich or something easy. Oh, and Charlie says cataracts are no problem. You can be in and out of hospital on the same day and can see properly in a day or two. So no more excuses. You must go to the doctor as soon as possible.'

Audrey stopped in her tracks and turned around slowly to face Rachel.

'What? You've been discussing me with other people? How dare you? It's nobody's business but mine.'

'For goodness' sake, Mum, it was only Charlie. I haven't exactly broadcast it on national radio. Anyway, if it is a cataract and you get it treated soon, it's a relatively minor operation. If you leave it, you could lose the sight in the eye permanently. So do it, Mum. I mean it. While I'm here.'

'You've still got no right to discuss me with anyone else. Now, please go and put Binkie in the house and then come back here to help. Your father's gone to the bank, so I could do with another pair of hands.'

Silently Rachel left the shop and went along the drive to the cottage to put Binkie back in her bed. The cat scowled at her and then deliberately turned her back on her.

'Honestly! You're as bad as Mum. Just as stubborn.'

Maybe she *had* been wrong to mention her mother's health problem outside the family, but she'd had the best of intentions and she was very worried about her.

★ ★ ★

Rachel wandered around the shop for the rest of the morning, wondering what to do with herself. There were no customers, and she'd tidied everything to within an inch of its life. Maybe it was time to visit some sales and buy some fresh stock.

If her dad held the fort, then she and her mum could have a day or two at the auctions. Maybe that would cheer up Audrey.

But when Rachel suggested this, her mother wasn't at all enthusiastic and made a comment about not wanting to waste any more money than was necessary.

Rachel stared at her in surprise.

'You and Dad are all right financially, aren't you, Mum? The business isn't in trouble, is it?'

'Well, not as such. But it isn't doing as well as in the past. People don't seem to have money to spend on our sort of stuff at the moment. So, no, we're not in trouble, but . . . well, we're not getting any younger and you'd never want to take this business over. Not with your life in London and your career as a media consultant.'

'But suppose I did move back here? What would you think of that?'

'You're joking! Why on earth would you do that? You've got your flat and everything. And what about your job? I thought you loved it?'

'Like I said the other day, I'm thinking of quitting the job. The media business is getting too cut-throat for my liking. There are too many new graduates all going for the same jobs. I really needed a long break and I had to fight to take even my allotted holiday. I've been working all the hours possible and that still isn't enough for my bosses. As for the flat, it's only rented, and the girl I share with has another friend who might take it on if I give notice. I thought if I stayed down here for a while, then I could look around for a new job and see a bit of my parents while I'm doing it.'

'I see. So what are you saying? That you plan to stay indefinitely?'

'Maybe. I'll contribute to the expenses, of course. I've got some savings.'

'Don't be silly, dear. You're helping

out in the shop. That's contribution enough.'

'Not if you're trying to cut back. We'll discuss this some more with Dad. Look, I think that couple are coming in. Get some coffee going and the smell will surely tempt them to linger.'

There was a steady trickle of customers throughout the rest of the morning, most of them having coffee and scones, but none of them interested in buying antiques of any sort.

Soon Jack returned from the bank.

'How are my best girls doing?' he asked.

'It's been rather quiet, I'm afraid. Binkie's been to the vet and had a jab and some cream, and Rachel's going out with Charlie this evening. And she says she's planning to stay at home for a while.'

'I see. Doesn't actually sound like the quietest of mornings. So, you've met up with Charlie Williams again, have you, lovey?' he said with a wink at his daughter.

'Da-ad,' she chided. 'Yes, I met him again. He's still nice and still friendly. But like I said to Mum, it's just a drink. Don't go getting ideas.'

'And she had the cheek to tell him I have problems with my eyes. Can you credit that, Jack? Discussing my medical problems with the vet!'

'Well, you *do* have problems.'

'Nothing I can't manage. But to tell the world and his wife!'

'She just told Charlie. Methinks the lady doth protest too much,' he teased as he put his arms around her middle. 'If you won't take advice from the vet, then why not do as we keep telling you and go to the doctor?'

'Not you, too! Please, can't you leave me alone? It's nothing!'

'If it's nothing, then there's nothing to fear from the doctor, is there?' Rachel said. 'Anyone want a sandwich if I go and make some?'

'No need! I brought us a treat,' her father announced. 'Pasties all round.'

'Great,' Rachel enthused. 'About

time I tasted the local delicacy again. Are they from Porters'?'

'Of course. They're doing them frozen now and they supply several shops in the area. They even provide a special oven that cooks them quickly, so anyone can sell them.'

'Are you going to?'

'Well, I was wondering if we might,' he replied thoughtfully. 'Trouble is, we're turning into a teashop rather than an antiques shop.'

'Maybe it's the way to go. You had to get clearance from food hygiene for the cream teas, so there shouldn't be a problem expanding that side of your trade.'

Rachel noticed how her parents looked at each other and frowned. She saw how her mother shook her head at Jack and then turned away to busy herself with some washing up.

'Is there something the two of you aren't telling me?' Rachel demanded.

But her parents had closed ranks and she could get nothing more from them.

Instead, the three of them sat down at one of the shop tables and had just begun to tuck into the delicious pasties when two young men with large backpacks came into the shop.

'Oh, great! Pasties! Can we have a couple, please?' one of the boys asked eagerly.

'I'm sorry. This is our lunch. We don't actually sell them.'

'That's too cruel. We're starving. Haven't you got anything we can eat?'

'We really only do cream teas. But I could do you a sandwich if you like?'

'Well, thanks for the offer, but is there anywhere else around here where we could get hot pasties?'

'Afraid not,' Rachel told them. 'As a matter of fact, we were just discussing the possibility of starting to sell them in here. But the next village is the nearest place you'll get hot pasties today. Or there's the pub?'

'OK, then. Thanks. Boy, do they smell good! But I guess we'll just have to go and see what the pub has to offer.'

'See?' Rachel said triumphantly after the lads had left the shop. 'There's an instant market for this kind of food.'

'Possibly, but I'm not sure it's what we want to do,' her father told her.

'Well, we sure need to do something to boost trade,' insisted Rachel. 'I've been thinking. If I'm going to be at home for some time then I ought to invest in a laptop computer. That way we can deal with our stock on the Internet. You'd be amazed what you can buy and sell in cyberspace. It's like holding a personal auction in your own living-room. In fact, I think I should go to Truro this afternoon and buy one right away. I miss not having access to the world at large. You don't need me for a few hours, do you?'

'Of course not, love. You're on holiday. But should you be going to all that expense if you're thinking of giving up your work? You don't know how long it might take you to find a new job. And to be honest, I haven't a clue about the Internet. I'm totally fogged by it all. Computers and all that stuff — ' Audrey shook her head at the very thought.

'Don't you worry, Mum, you'll soon get to love it. And once I start dealing online, the laptop will pay for itself in no time. You'll see. Be back soon.'

She almost ran out of the shop.

'That girl rushes around so much she'll meet herself coming back one of these days,' Audrey said, shaking her head. 'She takes my breath away.'

'It'll have a big effect on us though, love, if she does give up her job. Having her home indefinitely could ruin our plans.'

'I suppose it could. Oh, dear. Just when things looked like they were going to sort themselves out, too.'

'We'll talk about it later. Take some time to think a bit more. I must say, it's all a bit unexpected. I never thought she'd come back to live at home, did you? Not for one minute. Now, are we having a cuppa? I'll put the kettle on, shall I?'

'Hmm . . . I don't know why, but I have the feeling there's something she's not telling us.'

'Oh, come on, love. You're never happy unless you've got something to worry over. And you never know — maybe something will come of this Charlie business. That would solve everything. We'd have our girl near us and we could still move to a bungalow.'

'If we can ever afford to, the way house prices are going.'

'Works both ways. If we get a decent price for both the shop and the cottage, then we should be in with a chance.'

'But we can hardly sell the business as a going concern. This past year, we've barely broken even.'

Jack made tea and persuaded his wife to sit down. He knew that — in spite of all her protestations — she was very concerned about her failing sight and that this worry, together with the problem of what to do about their failing business, was beginning to affect her health.

It began to rain.

'This will either drive folks home or inside for shelter,' Jack remarked. 'I'll make sure we've got plenty of hot water, just in case.'

'You're a good man, Jack Cranham.'

'And you're a very lovely woman, Audrey Cranham. If you weren't married, I'd be asking you out.'

They laughed fondly and she pressed his hand to her face.

'I'm a very *lucky* woman,' she corrected him. 'Now, do you reckon these people are about to come inside?'

'I do believe they are. Action stations.'

By the time they closed, a few more pounds had been added to the takings.

One couple had shown great interest in the child's chair that Rachel had placed in the window. While they'd been having their tea they'd debated whether or not to buy it but hadn't been able to make up their minds.

Jack was certain they'd be back for it. They'd said they had a new grandchild and had hesitated only because of carrying it back home with them.

'I'd miss it if it went,' Audrey had remarked. 'It's been here for so long.'

'Precisely,' Jack had said. 'And it's time we shifted it. You know, if we do sell up, we'll have to part with a load of old memories before we can move.'

'You're right. It is time we let things go.'

They shut the shop and went back to the cottage. Rachel had still not returned from her buying mission so Audrey got on with preparing supper.

★　★　★

It was six-thirty when Rachel eventually breezed in.

'I'm sorry. You wanted me to help, didn't you? I lost track of the time and, well, this is it what I was doing.'

She held out a large box to show them how she'd spent her afternoon.

'I got a really good deal with loads of extras thrown in. Just you wait till you see what it can do. Oh, and we'll need to sort something out about the phone but that won't be a problem.'

'I haven't a clue what you're talking about, love, but I'm sure it's all wonderful. Now, weren't you going out this evening? With Charlie? I've got supper on the go so if you want to get ready first, you can eat after. It's only something light. After the pasties at lunchtime, I didn't think we'd want much.'

Audrey was much more interested in her daughter's date with the vet than in the new computer. They'd lived without the Internet all their lives. Why should they suddenly need it now?

'But don't you at least want to look?' Rachel began unpacking the contents of the box on to the dining table.

'I think your mum's a bit worried about the time. You said Charlie was coming at half-past seven, didn't you? That gives you about forty-five minutes to get ready and have your meal.'

'Oh, Dad, don't fuss. It's only

Charlie. All right.' She held up her hands in surrender. 'I'll take this upstairs and go and change.'

'Water's hot if you want a shower,' her mother called.

'Not enough time. A quick wash and brush up will have to do. Won't be a moment. I'm starving.'

She rushed up the narrow stairs and they heard her clattering around, banging doors, and then the sound of running water.

'I feel exhausted just listening to her. I do hope she and Charlie hit it off. It would be very nice to have her settled down here near us.'

'But preferably not actually living with us?' suggested Jack.

'I don't know. Much as I love her, she's a bit of a hurricane to have at close quarters. Am I getting old?'

'Of course not. It's been a stressful few months with the business, though. If it doesn't pick up in the next few weeks, we'll have to make some harsh decisions. Say no more now.'

He'd heard Rachel coming down the stairs and didn't want any sort of discussion with her just yet.

'Come on, dear. It's cauliflower cheese.'

'Great. Just what I'd have chosen myself.'

Rachel tucked in and soon her plate was cleared.

'I might have a piece of your fruit cake now, Mum. I'm sure you've got one hidden away somewhere.'

'I don't know how you keep so slim,' her mother told her.

'I'm always on the go, that's how. Any more tea in the pot?'

'Pass your cup. Any idea where you're going?'

'No. Just somewhere for a drink. Probably the Beach Bar. I've lost touch with the best places around here. Charlie's sure to know where's cool.'

'Silly expression.'

'Don't be grumpy, Mum. I'll just go and brush my teeth. Gosh, it's good to be home and to get regular meals. So civilised to have real food in the cupboard, and a fridge that has more in it than a few limp lettuce leaves. See you.'

'Honestly. The things she says.'

'Come on, Audrey. She's right — you are turning into a 'grumpy old woman'.'

'Oh, Jack, I'm not, am I? Not really?'

'Just a saying. Relax. I'll clear the table and you can go and put your feet up. You'll be just in time for your favourite soaps.'

'Thanks, love.'

The doorbell rang and Rachel pounded down the stairs.

'I've got it! See you both later.'

'Don't you want to ask Charlie in for a drink . . . ' Audrey tailed off as the door slammed. 'Oh, well, at least I get to see the telly without interruptions,' she said with a sigh.

A Disappointment
For Rachel

The large four-wheel drive vehicle was parked out in the road. Charlie was standing by it, waiting for Rachel to join him.

'Hi, there! Sorry I didn't wait at the door for you, but strictly speaking, I'm illegally parked here.'

'That's quite a motor. Bit of a change from your old Mini.'

'I need this for the business. Farm visits and all that. You'd be amazed at what I need to carry. Mind you, we did all right with that old Mini, with both the surf boards strapped to the roof.'

Rachel laughed. 'And, lots of the time, five of us inside with all our gear. You were so privileged to have your own transport.'

'Yes, but I worked very hard for that

car. The hours I spent cleaning out animal cages and chopping up unmentionable stuff for feed.'

A van came along the road and hooted as it tried to pass.

'Jump in and we'll decide where to go. I didn't have time for supper — do you want to go somewhere to eat?' Charlie suggested.

'Well, I've just had something but I can always have a snack just to keep you company.'

Charlie started the car and drove off towards the coast road.

'You haven't changed! I seem to remember you always liked your food. You've somehow managed to stay slim despite having a labourer's appetite.'

She punched his arm in a friendly way, grinning as she did so. They may have grown up but there was still a closeness between them.

'You haven't changed all that much,' she said happily. 'Despite the years away at university and everything else you must have done.'

'Oh, I think I've changed a lot. So have you. Much more sophisticated, for a start. No ripped denim shorts and ratty T-shirts.'

'I should say not! What would you have said if I'd turned up looking like that? I'm twenty-six, for heaven's sake. Not a teenager any more.'

'I'd have been appreciative of the skimpy clothes, of course. But I see what you mean. I like your hair longer, too. Suits you. You used to have it cut really short. Shorter than mine at one time, I seem to remember.'

'It made it easier when we were in and out of the sea all the time.'

They smiled together at fond memories.

'Now, do you fancy the noisy Beach Bar with all the youngsters or shall we be more grown-up?'

'Oh, dear. I don't really fancy the Beach Bar. Have we really grown up so much?'

'I certainly have. Got responsibilities now. A proper career and all. You?'

'Well, I'm thinking of a change. Of career, I mean. I'm sick of the London rat race. I need something that's more sincere, if you understand what I mean. Somehow, it seems all rush and pressure, and if you slow down there's always someone ready to stab you in the back. Well, maybe not that dramatic, but you can't ever really relax.'

'I do understand, and it sounds dreadful. But what will you do? You work at some sort of media agency, don't you?'

'Did. I haven't quite got round to telling my parents but I've already resigned and cleared my desk. I've only told Mum and Dad that I'm thinking about leaving my job. I was sort of planning to join them working in the shop for a while. Do a bit of trading on the Internet.'

'They'd never go for that, would they? I mean, they're both real 'people' people. They're so good at it. They enjoy the interaction with the customers. Besides, could the business actually support all of you?'

Rachel suddenly felt uneasy. She'd sensed a slight tension in her parents when she'd spoken about the shop but they'd denied anything was wrong. Maybe Charlie had heard some gossip in the village.

They stopped outside a small pub and he grinned at her.

'This is all new for you, isn't it?' she suggested. 'The quiet country pub and a proper career.'

'Like I said, I've grown up.'

★ ★ ★

They both enjoyed their evening together. The old familiar ease was still there between them. They laughed together, and chatted about old times as well as about what they'd both been doing in the intervening years.

Charlie had clearly found his niche and was loving his work and life in Cornwall.

'So how come you're still single?' Rachel asked.

Charlie hesitated.

'Oh, I'm sorry! Maybe you're not! I just assumed you were, since you'd asked me out.'

'I am still single, in as much as I'm not married, but I'm — well, involved with someone.'

'Oh.' She felt suddenly bereft. 'Who is she? Someone I know? Someone local?'

'No. She works in Bristol. She's a university lecturer. Albeit a junior one.'

'Wow. That's good going. Assuming she's our age.'

'She's a bit older than me, actually,' he confided with a small smile.

'And are you engaged?'

Rachel found her voice was slightly shaky and she felt a sense of loss creeping over her. Charlie had a girlfriend and she was shocked to find that she felt very jealous of this unknown woman.

'We have a sort of understanding. I suppose we've both assumed we'll get engaged one day. I think you'd like her. You must meet her next time she comes down here.'

'That would be nice,' Rachel said without enthusiasm.

She pushed the remains of her roll to one side. Her appetite had gone, along with her pleasure at spending an evening with her one-time best friend.

'And what about you, Rachel? I'd expected you to be settled down by now with a trail of toddlers.'

'You're kidding! No, I've not found anyone yet that I want to settle down with. I've had boyfriends, of course, but nobody special. You set quite a high standard in your day.'

He blushed.

She'd forgotten his propensity to blush and found it quite endearing. How could she have expected him still to be unattached? He was such an attractive man . . . even more attractive than the boy she had once known.

'So, how often do you see your fiancée?'

'She's not my fiancée. Like I said, we just have an understanding. She comes down for the occasional weekend and I go to her place at other times.'

'And what's her name?'

'Gemma. We met at university.'

'I see. So she's a vet, too? Or presumably lectures in the subject?'

'Not at all. She's an archaeologist. Often to be found crawling down a muddy hole somewhere! Completely different course to mine but, well, I got involved with some conservation work and that's how we met. But enough about me. Tell me about your life. You must have loved being in London. I remember you always wanted to experience city life — theatres and clubs and all that.'

'Oh, I enjoyed it for a while. But I've always loved Cornwall, and one day I realised I'd had enough of the constant noise and rush of London. I wanted to smell the sea instead of traffic fumes. I wanted to walk along the cliff tops and have time to slow down and really look at things again. As I said before, in the London media business if you relax for a moment then you find someone else has crept in with a new idea and the boss prefers that to what you were working on. But, of course, I do worry a bit about what I'm going to do next. Maybe you're right about Mum and Dad's shop. It wouldn't support us all.'

'Perhaps they'd retire and let you run it.'

'I doubt they could afford to. They've never exactly made a fortune so I doubt they've saved much. But I've got enough put by to last me a few months, so there's plenty of time for me to look around for another job.'

'Let's have another drink. Then I suppose we'd better push off. I have an early start tomorrow.'

Rachel watched him as he went up to the bar. Though his shoulders were broad, he was slim around the waist and seemed taller than she remembered. She realised she was feeling more than a little sad that he was settled with someone. Even if it was what he called just an *understanding*, he'd clearly made some sort of commitment to this Gemma.

Maybe she'd allowed her mother's enthusiasm to colour her own thoughts. She had to admit that she'd had higher hopes herself of this evening than merely catching up with Charlie, her old boyfriend from so long ago.

'There you are,' he said cheerfully, putting the drinks on the table. 'Cheers. I can't tell you how much I've enjoyed seeing you again and having a good natter about the old days. We must do it again. I plan to see plenty of you while you're home — I can't actually believe you'll really stay on here so I'll make the most of you before you disappear off into the wild blue yonder once more.'

'That would be nice, but how would your Gemma feel about that?'

He gave a shrug and pursed his lips.

'She doesn't expect me to stay at home every night. And you and me, well, we're old mates. Go back a long way, don't we?'

'Well, we certainly go back a long way, I have to agree with you on that. But 'old mates'? That makes what we used to have between us sound very casual.'

Charlie stared at her.

'Well, it was, wasn't it? We spent a lot of time together when we were kids. I suppose you could have called it going out together but it was always with a crowd. Nothing too serious. We were both hellbent on university and getting ourselves careers and stuff in those days.'

Now it was Rachel's turn to blush. Obviously Charlie had never realised just how much he meant to her. It seemed that to him, she had only ever been someone to hang around with. One of the gang.

She thought back to their shy kisses behind the boat sheds. Her first real boyfriend, or so she'd thought. A sign that she was growing up. That she was beginning her life as a woman.

But to Charlie, she had obviously been merely an experiment in moving on from his adolescent immaturity.

She quickly finished her drink and picked up her bag.

'So, are you ready to go?'

'Yes. Is anything wrong?' he asked curiously.

'Not at all. I'm just a bit tired. The Cornwall effect. Everyone says they feel sleepy after a few days here. Must be the slower pace of life.'

'I wish I could live life at a slower pace some days. I sometimes think that mobile phones are the bane of my life. I know they're a blessing in many ways but the fact that anyone can reach me on my phone at any time makes it difficult to have a social life.'

'It's been silent enough tonight.'

'I switched it off,' he confessed. 'Dad's at home so he could pick up any calls. I didn't want our evening spoilt with some horse or cow needing my attention.'

'Well, at least I rate more highly than a sick cow. I suppose that's something.'

'Rachel, what on earth do you mean by that?'

'Nothing. Joke. It was a joke.'

He stared at her and opened the door to usher her out. Silently they walked back to his car.

'Have I said something to upset you?' he asked, as he put the key in the ignition. 'Only you've suddenly gone all strange on me.'

'Like I said, I'm tired. I've had a stressful few weeks and, well, I guess it was a bit emotional seeing you again and realising we'd both grown up so much in the last few years.'

He reached out and took her hand, squeezing it gently.

'It's quite hard when you realise things are changing, isn't it? It's gradual until you suddenly realise that nothing is quite the same as it was. My dad's been going through that lately. He was thrilled when I agreed to go into partnership with him, and then he wasn't well at one point so I took on more and more of the work. Now he's semi-retired and just does the odd clinic and practically no visits. He doesn't quite believe I'm capable of managing everything. Well, I admit I'm still young for such responsibility and I'm extremely lucky to get the opportunity. But I do remember to ask his advice quite often, of course.'

'Maybe that's happening to my parents too. I suppose they're all about the same age. Our parents, I mean. I was born when Mum was well into her thirties, when they'd just about given up hope of ever having a child.'

Charlie started the car.

Both were busy with their thoughts and memories as he drove the few miles back to the village.

Rachel felt oddly disturbed as they pulled up outside the little shop.

Cranhams' Curios was in darkness and looked rather forlorn.

'We do need to cheer this place up, don't we?' she said. 'We need to do something to draw people to look inside. Maybe some lights in the window would help.'

'Let's go out again soon,' Charlie suggested.

She hesitated. Much as she wanted to say yes, she sensed that it might lead to heartache. They say you never forget your first love.

She shook herself back into reality. She had only just met him again and here she was fantasising about a future that could never exist. She realised he was saying something and that she'd missed it entirely.

'Well, what do you think?'

'Erm . . . I'm not sure.'

'Please — say you'll go out again with me.'

'I'd like to but . . . I mean, I'd hate to cause you any problems. With Gemma.'

'Come on — she's hardly going to object if I see something of an old friend. Besides, you may not be here for very long and we've still got loads to talk about.'

'Well, if you're sure. OK.'

'You don't sound madly enthusiastic! But I've enjoyed this evening, even if you haven't! I'll give you a call, will I? And we'll arrange to meet up again. Actually, I'll leave the ball in your court. You can call me.'

'OK. And thanks for a lovely evening,' she told him politely. 'Seriously, it's been lovely to see you. And of course I'd like to go out with you again.'

He reached over and gave her a peck on the cheek.

She jumped in surprise. If she'd realised what he'd been about to do, she might not have turned away and the kiss might have found a better target.

''Bye then. I'll wait for your call.'

She watched as he drove away and then she walked up the little drive.

The security light came on, illuminating the garden. She spotted a rabbit darting back into the undergrowth and smiled. Her father fought a constant battle against the rabbits that seemed to eat everything in sight. They scraped up the lawn and ate the tops off the flowers he planted.

It was good to be home among familiar sights. She didn't think she would miss London at all. But what on earth was she going to do with herself if she didn't work in the shop?

She let herself in.

'Is that you, Rachel?' called her mother from upstairs.

'Yes, of course it is!'

'I've left you a coffee tray in the kitchen. Is Charlie with you?'

'No. I never thought to ask him in. Besides, he had an early start. But thanks for the thought. I'll make myself a cup and take it up to bed. Goodnight.'

'I hope you had a nice evening, dear. Sleep well.'

Rachel heard her mum go back into her bedroom and shut the door.

Then she made herself a milky drink and, ignoring her mother's carefully set tray, poured it into a mug and took it to her room where she sat on her bed and nursed the mug between her hands, thinking about her evening.

Everything had been going well until Charlie had mentioned Gemma. A lecturer. Archaeology, he'd said. She was probably very bright and much more dynamic than Rachel could ever be. You didn't get to be a lecturer at such a young age if you weren't both of those things.

But it was so foolish to feel jealous. Rachel and Charlie had shared good times in the past and that's just where they were. In the past. Whatever romantic feelings she might once have had were childish dreams and best forgotten.

But he was still fun to be with and there was absolutely no reason not to see him again if he wanted to spend time with her.

She sipped her drink and forced herself to think more positively.

She really must speak to her parents about her own prospects and about whether she had a future in the shop, working with them.

She glanced at her new laptop computer.

Tomorrow she would spend some time online, looking for new stock. She might even put some of the old stock on one of the auction sites on the Internet. It was a growing trend everywhere, so maybe it would work for her parents' shop.

★　★　★

Over breakfast the next morning, Rachel explained to her mum and dad how she intended to use the new computer to help their business. Her mother was much more interested in hearing about her evening out but Rachel was unwilling to be drawn on that subject. She persisted in explaining her plans.

'It sounds interesting, dear,' Jack agreed, 'but I don't really think it's relevant to us down here in Cornwall.'

'But that's the whole point, Dad. Using the computer, we gain access to the entire world. We can advertise items for sale and people anywhere and everywhere can find the advert and bid for the things. Let's give it a try.'

'I suppose it does no harm,' Audrey said. 'I don't understand any of it, of course, but if you know what you want to do, go ahead and do it. You agree, Jack?'

Jack Cranham nodded and Rachel grinned.

'OK, I'll get on to it this morning. Let's look round the shop. I shall need to take pictures of whatever we plan to sell.'

'There may be a film in the old camera but I can't guarantee it will still come out all right.'

'It's OK, I've got a digital camera. We can put the pictures straight on to the laptop.'

Audrey grimaced. 'Oh, dear, we seem to live in completely different worlds with digital this and that everywhere. I feel like I've been left behind — that I'm as out of date as the antiques in the shop! Tell you what, I'll go and make the scones. At least I can still do that.'

'You certainly can, love,' Jack said fondly. 'Nobody comes near your standard of baking. You go and open up and I'll clear away the dishes here.'

'Thanks, Dad,' Rachel said when her mother had left the room. 'I hope I'm not messing you around at all. Coming back, I mean?'

'Of course not, love. We're pleased to have you here. Always are. How long a holiday have you got?'

'Well, actually, this is a bit more than a holiday. I didn't want to worry you straight away, but I've already left my job at the agency. I really don't want to work in London any more.'

'Good heavens. I hope you won't regret it! What about your flat and everything?'

'I have to go back and clear out my stuff in a week or so. But I needed to know it would be all right to stay here with you and Mum for a while.'

'What do you propose to do next?'

'I thought I might work here in the shop for a while. Take some of the pressure off you and Mum. That's OK, isn't it?'

'Well, Rachel,' he said, frowning, 'I need some time to think about it. You've quite flummoxed us, to be honest. We've never imagined you living at home again, let alone wanting to work in the shop!'

'The business is all right, isn't it?'

'Oh, everything's fine,' he confirmed absently. 'I'd better get over there. Your mum will wonder what's happened to us. Look, let's give it a bit of time, eh? Time to think and plan.'

'Sure,' she said. She was puzzled. She'd expected her parents to be delighted at the prospect of them all working together for a while but clearly there was something wrong.

Something they didn't want her to know about.

Big Plans!

Rachel spent some time unpacking her new computer and learning how to set it all up. Then, once she'd familiarised herself with its operation, she went over to the shop, carrying it carefully with her.

'I thought I'd see if you needed any help?' she said.

'We're fine. Another quiet day. I'm just hoping things will waken up at Easter.' Her mother was looking slightly worried.

'It usually does, dear,' Jack said comfortingly. 'We say it every year when the first trickle of visitors starts to arrive.'

'Well, since you've got time, maybe you'd like to have a look at my new toy?' suggested Rachel. 'I've got it all set up and ready to go. I just need to plug it into the telephone socket. I think we'll have to get an adaptor or something. Anyway, for now it can go in here.'

She reached over the counter, unplugged the shop phone and pushed in her computer's connection.

'Hang on — suppose someone tries to ring us? They won't be able to get through, will they?' Audrey asked.

'They'll get the engaged tone. But it won't be for long. I just want to show you the auction site, so you'll get the idea.'

'It's very small, isn't it, your machine? Only about as big as two books side by side. I don't understand how it works at all,' her father said.

'Nor do I, but I know how to work *it*. That's all that matters. I leave all the complicated stuff to the experts. It's like a very complicated television in a way. You know how to work the television — switch programmes and everything, don't you? But you have no idea how the insides of the thing work, do you?'

'True,' he agreed.

'And if something goes wrong, you call in the experts!'

She tapped away at the keyboard, keying in the web address of the online auction site, and a moment later, brightly-coloured photographs filled the screen.

'See? If I type in a description, here in this little box, of something we want to buy, then we get a list of all the people who are selling whatever it is that we're looking for. What *shall* we look for?'

'I don't know. I'm not really interested in all this technology stuff. I think I'd better go and make some sandwiches.' Audrey really didn't want to be bothered by it all.

'Oh, Mum. Please give it a go. Let's type in 'Clarice Cliff'.'

Rachel did so, and a list of over a thousand items appeared. She made one of the items come up on the screen in detail.

'Oh, my goodness!' Audrey exclaimed.

'Just look at that jam pot! It's four hundred pounds. I sold one in the shop not so long ago and got fifteen pounds for it. Mind you, it wasn't in such good condition or in such a popular design. And it did have a crack in it. But all the same, somebody got a bargain. Can you look up something else?' She looked around the shop, scanning the displays. 'What about that little Beswick horse on the dresser over there?'

Delighted by her mother's sudden interest, Rachel typed 'Beswick Horse' into the little box at the top of the screen. A new list of about one hundred items appeared and Audrey gave a huge sigh.

'Well, if there are so many of these things for sale, no wonder we're hardly doing any trade. We might as well close down right now and give up trying.'

'It does make our little shop seem a bit pointless,' Jack agreed.

'But don't you see? We can put our own stock into the sale. You might get lots more money for things selling them online than you do in the shop. And people will be logging in to buy from all over the world! What do you think? Shall we give it a try? I can take one or two photographs and put them on this site and we can see what happens.'

'If you like, dear. If you think it can work and you know what to do. But it's still all a mystery to me.'

Rachel looked pleased. 'I'll get on with taking the pics then!'

She unplugged the computer and plugged the phone back in.

It rang almost immediately.

'Hello, Cranhams' Curios,' Audrey answered, looking annoyed at the thought that someone had been phoning and might not have been able to get through. 'Oh, Marjorie. How are you? Yes. Oh, you didn't? I'm so sorry. Oh, you poor thing. Is it very painful? Is there anything I can do? No, it's no trouble. I've got Rachel home and she's busy organising us. Yes, that's why the phone was engaged. She's got a computer and was showing us how it works. It needs a telephone of its own apparently. I know — terrifying! I'll see you later. Can I bring anything for you? OK. I'll just write it down. Pen, Jack, please. Right — right — yes, I can get that, no problem. Now just you take it easy. 'Bye.'

'Something wrong?' Jack asked.

'Marjorie's sprained her wrist. She's in a bit of a state. I said I'd go round later and take her one or two bits of shopping. You won't mind holding the fort, will you?'

'Give her my love,' Rachel said. 'I haven't seen her for ages.'

Marjorie was one of Audrey's oldest friends; the two women had known each other since before Audrey had married Jack. Marjorie was several years older than her but that had never bothered either of them, and they still got together regularly for a cup of tea and a good old gossip.

'By the way, she said she'd been trying for ages to get through on the phone. You mustn't block the line again, Rachel — make some other arrangement, please.'

'I'll use the laptop in the house when the shop's open. That way there won't be any conflict. Maybe we'd better get broadband installed,' Rachel muttered thoughtfully.

'I've no idea what you're talking about but you won't be getting anything installed that costs money. Not until we see if this idea of yours is really going to work.'

'Don't worry, I'll pay for it if we need it.'

'Does this mean you're definitely staying on here for a while?' Audrey demanded.

'Well, yes. But only if you're happy with the idea.'

'Of course we'd be delighted to have you home again. But we thought you were so happy in London. This seems such a big decision for you to make on a whim.'

Audrey peered at her daughter anxiously.

'Well, actually, I haven't made up my mind on a whim. It's something I've been thinking of doing for a long time. Living in London and working for a big media agency isn't as glamorous and exciting as you might think it is — or as I thought it was going to be. It's just very hard work. So, I came to a big decision a while back. I've already left my job, and with my savings to keep me going, I thought I'd take time out to look for something else down here in Cornwall. If I can stay with you for a while, it will give me a bit of breathing space.'

'Oh, good heavens. What about your flat?'

'As I mentioned to Dad, I need to go back next week to clear out my stuff. It's only rented, of course, and someone else wants my room — a friend of Dawn's from her work. So it's all worked out well!'

'Looks like you've got it sorted then.' Audrey put her arms around Rachel and gave her a big hug. 'Well, I must say, I never expected our little girl to come back home again.'

'I suppose it does seem a bit like giving up and going backwards. But I'll soon find something, and meantime, I can help out here. And, Mum — you can get your eyes seen to.'

'Oh, not that again. I'm all right, I tell you. Now get on both of you. Get out of my way for five minutes.'

Rachel picked up her laptop and took it back to the cottage. Then, after collecting her camera, she returned to the shop to take photographs of a variety of small items that she thought would sell easily online. She arranged each piece of stock carefully to get the best light and took several shots of everything, from various angles.

'Aren't you wasting rather a lot of film?' Audrey asked.

'It's a digital camera, Mum. It doesn't use film. I'll show you the pictures later. On the computer. Now, you'll have to take these things off display until the auction ends. We don't want anyone to buy them before they've had a chance to attract bids. Hey, I've had an idea! We could make a special display on one of the shelves in here and put up a notice explaining that they're up for auction and giving a reference to the site. And I'll need to design a website for the shop itself. Take pictures of everything. Yes — this is really interesting. You don't need me to help out in here this morning, do you?'

'Well, I was going round to see poor Marjorie, as you know. So you might need to give your dad a hand if he needs it.'

'No problem. I'll hang around in here this morning taking pictures ready for when I need them for the website later. I can easily stop if we should get a rush of customers.'

★   ★   ★

Shortly after Audrey had left to visit her friend, a couple who had come in for tea and scones asked why Rachel was taking so many photographs around the shop, and Jack told them proudly that she was setting up a website. 'Whatever that means,' he added with a wry smile.

'What a good idea!' the man said. 'Isn't modern technology amazing? Just think, we'll be able to sit at home and look at your shop via our computer long after our holiday here is over. What's your web address?'

'What do you mean?' Jack said with a frown. 'I've got a card here with the shop address and phone number.'

'No, Dad,' interrupted Rachel, 'the gentleman's asking for the address of our website.' She turned to speak to the couple, who had by now finished their cream teas and were getting up from their table, ready to leave. 'I haven't actually registered the name of the site yet. But just type in Cranhams' Curios and I'm sure you'll find it. And keep in touch — we're planning all sorts of innovations,' she told them.

'Great. You've got some nice things

for sale in here. Maybe we'll take another look around, eh, darling?'

His wife nodded and the two of them spent several minutes looking around the smaller items of bric-a-brac before settling on a pair of china cups and saucers.

Jack wrapped them carefully, and chatted to them for a while about holidays and local beauty spots.

'Thanks so much,' the wife said. 'We may be back to sample some more of your delicious scones before we leave Cornwall. I'd like to visit your village museum, too, before we head back home. And good luck with the website,' she added.

After they'd gone, Rachel gave her father a big grin.

'See, Dad? We've already got people interested. I'll drag you kicking and screaming into the twenty-first century yet!'

'No doubt you'll do whatever you want, love. You usually do! But I'll never understand all this technology.'

★ ★ ★

Rachel spent the rest of the morning planning her project. She took more pictures of the inside of the shop and decided she needed one of her mother holding a plate of fresh scones and maybe one of both parents standing outside the shop. She was excited and motivated and felt a rush of the sort of enthusiasm that had been missing from her life in London for a very long time. She gave her father an unexpected hug as she passed him and he looked pleased and surprised.

'I think you're just the breath of fresh air we needed, love. Things have been a bit depressing lately. Business is usually slow between Christmas and Easter, but for the past few weeks trade has been virtually none existent. It's been ridiculous. So, what with that and your mum's eyesight problems, well . . .'

'Dad, you really must help me to persuade her to get her eyes treated. It's a small operation and she'd be so much better afterwards.'

'You know your mum. But we'll work on her together and see what happens. Just take it easy. You know what she's like: needs to reach decisions by herself, and if we push too much, she'll only dig her heels in all the more.'

'You know Mum really well, don't you, Dad? Is that the reason for your success? I mean, you've been married for ever and still seem as fond of each other as ever.'

'Don't you ever let on, but we get on so well because I usually let her think she's thought of any ideas herself. That way, I can seem to give way to her. It's a case of planting the idea subtly in the first place. But I doubt you know much about subtlety. You're like a mini tornado!'

'Maybe I should try to take a few tips from you. I think most of my relationships have ended through my own impatience. I want too much to happen too quickly.'

'So, how did your evening out go with Charlie?'

'It was lovely to see him, but it won't be going anywhere. He's practically engaged to a woman he met at university. She's an archaeologist — a lecturer — living in Bristol, but although they have a long-distance relationship, they seem to be pretty serious.'

'I see. And that's disappointing for you?'

'Maybe. Just a bit. I always did have a soft spot for him. But, ever onwards. No use moping. And he's asked me out again.'

'Is that wise, if he's got someone else?'

'He thinks it's fine. We were never more than *mates* in his eyes.'

'Don't give yourself any more complications than you need in your life, lovey. If you can be mates, as you put it, I suppose there's no problem. But don't get hurt, or hurt anyone else in the process.'

'Thanks, Dad. Wise as ever.'

Audrey came back into the shop before they could say any more.

'You're looking very solemn,' she commented, sounding suspicious. 'Something wrong?'

'Of course not. Just chewing over life's mysteries.'

'Now I *am* worried!'

'Never mind us. How's Marjorie?' asked Jack, quickly changing the subject.

'Oh, poor Marjorie's in quite a state. She can't lift anything and she seems to be in such pain. She's having problems with the simplest things. Do you know, she said it took her half an hour just to get dressed? I said I'd go round again tomorrow and help her with her housework and do a bit of washing for her. Can you two manage without me?'

They both agreed that it was no problem.

'I hate this getting older business,' Audrey grumbled. 'You never know when your body's going to let you down. And if you're like Marjorie, and live on your own, how are you supposed to manage to look after yourself if you can only use one arm?'

'At least Marjorie's got plenty of money to manage on. Hasn't she got someone to help her in the house on a regular basis anyway?'

'Well, yes, she has that Janice Perkins going in to help her most days, but can you believe that Janice's little granddaughter's been taken ill, so she's gone to look after her while the child's mum goes to work. Timing, eh? But it makes you realise how old age creeps up on you.'

'Now, Mum, Marjorie's a good deal older than you, so don't go getting depressed about it. And are you sure you can manage to help her? I mean, what with your own health problems and everything.'

'I don't know what you mean, 'my health problems'! I suppose you're talking about my eyes again? I keep telling you, I'm fine. Now, what are we having for lunch today?'

*　　*　　*

Rachel spent that afternoon over in the cottage, sorting out her pictures, and was just about to plug her computer into the phone socket when the phone rang.

She frowned, irritated by an interruption that prevented her from getting on with what she wanted to do.

'Hello,' she said grumpily, expecting it to be one of her mother's friends on the line.

'Rachel? It's me.'

'Charlie! I thought I was supposed to call you first?'

'I decided not to risk waiting in case you didn't. Call, I mean.'

She felt ridiculously pleased at his words.

'So, why aren't you out saving the lives of sick animals?'

'I'm just having a break for a caffeine

fix and I thought I'd ring to say how good it was to see you last night.'

'It was good to see you, too.' She hoped her voice sounded steadier than it felt.

'I was wondering if you're free this evening?' Charlie went on. 'Last night we only scratched the surface of what we've been doing since we last met. We could have a proper bite to eat if you like?'

Rachel hesitated. Her heart screamed 'Yes please', but the sensible half of her said no, it wasn't a good idea to go out with Charlie again.

'That would be great,' she replied. 'Where do you want to go?'

'We can decide later. I'll pick you up around seven-thirty. Got to go. More sick pets arriving as I speak.'

'OK. See you later.'

She felt absurdly excited over her date that evening but tried hard to control her emotions. It was ridiculous. He had made it quite clear that she was just a friend and she must accept the situation, and besides, she didn't understand herself why he had suddenly become so important to her.

Taking a deep breath and trying to calm down, she went across to the shop to tell her parents she would be eating out that evening.

'Oh, how lovely!' her mother said with pleasure. 'He must be keen when he wants to see you again so soon.'

'Maybe. But to be honest, I think he's just at a loose end and wants to chat some more.'

'That's possible, I suppose,' her mum agreed. But she had a definite glint in her eye.

Rachel knew her mother would be delighted to see her married and settled down with a tribe of toddlers for her to coo over. It was a terrifying prospect . . . the toddlers, not the marriage.

★ ★ ★

Charlie and Rachel drove to a quiet little pub near the sea. It overlooked a pretty cove, and they sat in a window seat so that they could watch the crab fishers leaving port for their night's work. The little boats had riding lights and bobbed along on the water, leaving speckles of light shining in their wake.

It was a peaceful scene.

'I don't think I've been here before,' Rachel commented. 'It was a bit up-market for us in the old days, I suppose. We tended to go for the noisy, cheap and cheerful places, didn't we?'

Charlie smiled reminiscently.

'There wasn't so much choice in those days. I don't think quite so many places did food, anyhow. The best we ever afforded was a pizza between us, I seem to remember.'

She laughed softly and put her hand on his.

'Happy memories.'

'Now, what are you having? I'm told their fish is excellent . . . if you still like fish, that is?'

'Oh, I'm looking forward to some decent seafood. It never seems quite as good in London as it is here. Yes, I'll go for lemon sole.'

'Good choice. I'll have the same. And a bottle of Sauvignon Blanc?'

'Fine. Sounds much better than a cola and two straws.'

He went to the bar and placed the order, chatting away easily to the barman for a few minutes before he came back smiling.

'Seems I treated his daughter's rabbit a while back. He lives near St Truan and uses our practice. I can't go anywhere without being recognised these days.'

'Good job you've nothing to hide then. I guess you're probably a good vet. My mum swears by you, so you've at least one fan.'

'I like to think so. But I still have a lot to learn and we need to make some heavy investment in the practice. We need to update the equipment but Dad never wants to spend any money on upgrading. He thinks we should be able to manage just as he always had to.

Difficult to make anyone change their long-formed habits, isn't it?'

'Tell me about it.' She recounted her day of trying to get her parents interested in her ideas for selling antiques on the Internet. 'Honestly, you'd think I was suggesting parading through the streets with a banner and riding on the back of a white horse.'

'Hmm, that sounds an interesting idea. Lady Godiva style?'

They were both giggling as the barman arrived with their wine and glasses.

'Seriously though, it's an excellent idea to sell over the Internet. Everyone in business needs a website nowadays.'

''Those www things', as Mum calls them. Mind you, she was really shocked to see the prices some things can reach on the auction sites. I'm going to have a go at selling some of our old stock.'

They chatted as easily as before and could scarcely believe it when they realised it was almost eleven o'clock.

They'd both had puddings and coffee after the fish, and Rachel had drunk most of the wine, as Charlie was driving. She felt warm, contented and a little sleepy by the time they were on their way home.

'Do you want to come in for coffee?' she invited when he stopped to drop her off outside the shop. 'I was scolded for not asking you in last night.'

'Thanks, but I should get back. I've got surgery starting at eight in the morning, and a heavy day operating after that.'

'Well, thank you again. It's been a wonderful evening. I really enjoyed it and it was a lovely meal.'

'My pleasure. Thanks for your company.' He looked at her seriously. 'Rachel, I don't . . . '

'Hush, Charlie. I've had a really nice time. Don't spoil it.'

Not wanting a repeat of the peck on the cheek of the previous evening, she leaned over and kissed him lightly on the mouth.

He looked slightly startled but kissed her back.

'See you again?'

'Hope so.'

She went into the house feeling happier and more content than she had for ages. Her parents hadn't waited up and she heard them muttering through the closed door of their room.

She called goodnight and got ready for bed.

As she undressed, she wondered what they could be talking about so earnestly. She couldn't hear their words but the murmur of voices went on for some time.

If she had heard the words, she might have felt somewhat troubled by them.

Wet Feet!

'What are we going to do, love?' asked Audrey in worried tones. 'Let's face it, we're going to have to start planning all over again, thinking of a way we can afford to give up the shop and retire.'

'But how can we give up the shop and retire now that Rachel needs us to provide her with a roof over her head and somewhere to work?'

This conversation had been going backwards and forwards between them all evening, and was now continuing, long after they'd retired to bed for the night. Neither of them felt like sleeping and knew they couldn't, *wouldn't*, say any of these things in front of their daughter.

'It's a good job we hadn't already told her about our plans. She seems to need some time at home and if we'd told her we were planning to sell the shop and retire, she'd never have come here.'

'But much as we love her, it has altered everything, hasn't it? Oh, and I was so looking forward to moving to a modern bungalow — somewhere that's easy to clean and has no stairs to torment my rickety knees. I know we'd miss the shop and all the people coming and going, but we've been here all our married life and I'm just plain tired now.'

Apart from her problems with her sight, Audrey's arthritis was beginning to affect her more and more, and by the end of the day she sometimes felt as if she might drop.

'There are so many things we could do if we didn't have the shop,' agreed Jack. 'All those days out we promise ourselves every year and never get round to, for a start. But I don't expect Rachel will be here for long. Whatever she says, she'll get sick of the same old routine after a while and she'll be itching to get back to the bright lights.'

'But money's getting tighter and tighter all the time,' said Audrey. 'With the increase in council tax and business rates, we're barely holding our own. This new shop that's going to be opening along the road from here might just be the final straw. We can't go on for much longer. Not unless her crazy ideas with this computer work. I can't believe that Clarice Cliff jam pot made so much money!'

'Well, we have to give it a go for her sake. Though I doubt it's ever going to make us our fortunes here,' said Jack, with a sigh. 'Especially not with three of us hoping to make a living — even if we did start selling pasties and hot food. But we won't let on anything's wrong or even mention retirement plans for now. We don't want Rachel to feel she's being a nuisance. This is her home, after all. And I think we should keep quiet about the new Antiques and Craft Centre place or whatever it is that's supposed to be opening.'

'Agreed. Now we'd better try to get

some sleep. I heard her going to bed a while ago and she'll wonder what on earth is going on if we keep talking.' Audrey giggled. 'Reminds me of when she was little and had Chloe, that friend of hers over to spend the night. They'd be talking until all hours. I had to keep telling them to be quiet or Chloe would have to go home, middle of the night or not.'

Eventually, they both drifted off and the cottage was silent.

★　★　★

'Did you have a nice evening, then?' Audrey asked Rachel next morning when they were all having breakfast. She'd kept hoping Rachel would volunteer some information about her night out but had eventually had to give in and ask.

'Great. We went to that little pub — well, restaurant really — down by Leward Cove. It's lovely. You should go there one evening, you and Dad, for a treat.'

'Oh, I doubt your father would enjoy it. He likes home cooking and a peaceful life.'

'And your mother's usually worn out by the end of the day,' put in Jack.

'Anyhow, I like to sit and watch my favourite television programmes,' added Audrey.

'Just a suggestion,' Rachel said, staring at her parents. Time was they'd have leapt at the idea. She wondered once more if there was something going on that they hadn't told her about. 'You are both all right, aren't you?'

'Of course we are. Why wouldn't we be?'

Audrey exchanged a glance with Jack that didn't go unnoticed by their daughter.

'So, how were things with Charlie?'

'Good. Nice evening, as I said.'

'And you're seeing him again?'

'I expect so.'

'You were always quite fond of him, weren't you?'

'Leave it, love,' Jack told his wife.

'The poor girl doesn't want the equivalent of the Spanish Inquisition every time she goes out.'

Rachel shot him a grateful glance.

'I was only showing an interest,' complained Audrey.

'Right then,' interrupted Rachel, 'I'm going to put the things we decided to auction on to the site. Unless there's anything else you need help with?'

'No, there's not much going on.'

'Well, let's hope these plans come to fruition and we get some good results from it. Doesn't cost us anything except a few quid to set it up. No, don't look like that. I'm paying for it anyhow. Give me a call if you need me.'

'Oh, dear,' Audrey sighed after Rachel had left the shop to go back to the cottage. 'This is so difficult. We're beginning to sound like misers and we're penny watching like we're almost on the streets.'

Jack laughed. 'Well, I admit things aren't *that* bad. But all the same, I think we might consider selling some of our own antique bits and pieces from the cottage just to tide us over. We've got one or two good items of furniture that fill the place up but don't hold great sentimental value. If we do eventually move to a modern bungalow, we wouldn't want to take them with us anyhow.'

'You're right, but Rachel would be sure to guess that things aren't one hundred per cent here. We'll see what happens. You never know, this idea of hers might bring in some money. I just wish I understood half of what she's talking about. Oh, and what's all this silence about Charlie? She's been out with him two nights on the trot and yet she doesn't want to talk about him.'

'He's got a girlfriend. Rachel told me he's practically engaged.'

'So why's he messing our girl about?'

'He isn't. They're just — how did she put it? Mates. Yes, that was it.'

'And you really believe that for one minute? She always was sweet on him. And I like him, too. He's grown into a lovely young man and he's such a capable vet. He's wonderful with our Binkie. Such a change from the surfmad teenager he used to be. If only she could get herself nicely settled, it would make all the difference. Anyway, I'd better get on now. Haven't even got the coffee machine organised. I'm all behind this morning. And I must find time to go round to see how Marjorie is.'

Jack set about his usual morning tasks of dusting, cleaning, and labelling various things. He enjoyed pottering around his shop, just touching some of the things he particularly liked.

Audrey was in her own domain in the little kitchen, making scones and preparing for anyone who might call in for coffee.

She sighed occasionally as she worked, thinking of her daughter and the vet. It would be perfect if they could make a go of it.

In the meantime, with Rachel coming home to live on a more or less permanent basis, she had to resign herself to many more days of working in the shop and looking after the cottage with all its difficult-to-clean nooks and crannies, not to mention the steep, narrow stairs with the awkward corner.

But she loved her daughter dearly and knew she must forget her own dreams and simply enjoy the fact that Rachel was back to stay . . . at least for the time being.

★　★　★

In the cottage, Rachel was working at her computer and had selected three items to put on the auction site. She read all the rules and pressed the keys that would make it all happen.

Then she made herself some coffee and went back to the computer after a few minutes to check what was happening.

'Go on, then,' she muttered, 'someone else look at our stuff and put in a bid.'

Binkie got up, stretched, and gave a loud miaow before going to sprawl out on the sofa.

Rachel went over to peer at her ears.

'Are you better, cat, or do you need to go back to see the lovely Charlie?'

Binkie was going to be useful if Rachel didn't hear from Charlie again . . . the perfect excuse to go and see him.

She settled back to work and planned how to lay out the Cranhams' Curios website. Website design was something she'd done for some time as part of her job in London, so she had all the necessary skills.

She smiled as she thought about how wary her mother was of all things digital and technological. She didn't want anything to do with 'one of those www things everyone keeps talking about.'

Rachel had pointed out an advert in 'The People's Friend', one of her mother's favourite magazines, and had carefully explained that she could type the advertiser's website address into her laptop, and a page would come up on the screen which told her more about the item or company.

When she had completed their own page, her mother could look at it for herself and hopefully realise just how powerful a sales tool it could be.

She just needed a photograph of her parents standing together outside on the pavement in front of the shop window.

'Can you spare a minute?' she asked them, popping along the drive and in through the back door of the shop.

It was a needless question, really. With no customers in evidence, they so obviously could spare more than a minute.

'What is it, lass?' asked Jack, looking up from reading the paperback thriller he'd picked up to pass the time.

'I just need a nice shot of the two of you outside, with the shop in the background.'

'Oh, I'm in no state to have my picture taken. My hair's a mess and I'm in my old overall,' Audrey protested.

'You look fine,' Rachel argued. 'Take your pinny off and you'll be great. I want you to look natural anyway.'

'But what's it for?' her mother demanded to know.

'I'll show you later,' Rachel said quickly, not wanting to provoke even more questions.

They all went outside and she positioned her parents where she wanted them to stand. The sun was shining and the village was looking its best. One or two people walked past and looked at them with interest.

'You've such an obsession with photographs these days, our Rachel,' her mother complained. 'I don't know what all the fuss is about.'

'You'll see. Now, one or two extra interior shots and I'm done. Put some scones on a plate, Mum, and stand near the counter over there.'

Although they grumbled, both parents were intrigued and even flattered that she was taking so much trouble.

'How do you know what to do with all this stuff?' Audrey asked.

'It was my job. Well, part of it — making up pages for adverts and that sort of thing. Websites are the big thing these days — 'www things' to you, Mum.'

'So, we're really having one of those, are we?'

Rachel nodded and smiled.

'We're going to be 'www.cranhams-curios.com'.'

'Goodness me.'

'You know, I'm actually getting quite excited about all this,' Jack admitted. 'Do you think we should get on to the printers and get some new business cards made up with the new website address on them?'

'Oh, there's no need to do that! I'm going to print some for you once I've got some suitable card. I got a printer along with my laptop so we can run off all sorts of things. We could even make our own Christmas cards if we wanted to.'

'No more printing bills? That's just

great.' Audrey was showing a bit more interest now. 'And you can do it all for nothing?'

'Well, not quite. I have to buy special ink cartridges and paper and card. But it'll still be a lot cheaper than using a commercial printer. Right, well, if you don't need me for anything else, I'll go and sort this lot out.'

As she was making her way along the drive back to the cottage, a 'toot-toot' came from a passing car and she turned to see Charlie slowing down to speak to her.

'Hi. Lovely morning, isn't it?' he called out to her. 'None the worse for our evening out?'

'Of course not. Thank you again.'

'You taking up photography?' He indicated her camera.

'Just making a website for the shop. I wanted some shots of outside. Have you got time for a coffee?'

'Sorry, no. I must get to the Dimmocks' place. Sick heifer. See you soon. 'Bye.'

And he was gone.

She smiled to herself and then frowned. If he really was permanently out of her reach, it was going to be very difficult seeing him nearly every day. She would never get used to the way her heart started pounding whenever she saw him. Maybe she should try going out with someone else, just to settle things. The trouble was, there was nobody else around and certainly nobody she might choose to spend her evenings with.

She went back into the cottage and settled down to work.

Her father came over at lunchtime to make their usual sandwich lunch.

'Will you come over to join us, love? Then your mother wants to go and see Marjorie — if you don't mind staying in the shop for a bit. I've got a couple of errands to run.'

'I don't mind at all,' she replied, although secretly she was irritated to have been interrupted so near to finishing her task. Another couple of hours and she would be ready to launch the new site.

But it could always wait until the next day.

★ ★ ★

It was another quiet afternoon. There were one or two people drifting in and out of the shop but Rachel made no sales and she began to wonder if that was why her parents were so unwilling to spend any money. If this was typical of the sort of trade they were getting, they couldn't have much, these days, to spend.

She hoped the Internet auction would help boost their income, if only by a little.

Not having much to keep her occupied, Rachel fell to thinking about her future and decided she should really go to London to collect her things from the flat. She could contribute something to the family budget once she stopped paying rent for a place she wasn't using.

She resolved to call her flatmate that evening and make the arrangements.

★ ★ ★

'Any customers?' her mother asked hopefully when she returned from visiting her injured friend.

'I'm afraid not. How was Auntie Marjorie?'

'Not good at all. She's really down. She's even talking about selling up and moving into a nursing home.'

'Oh, surely not! She's got such a lovely place.'

'Yes, well, it's all too much for her now. She has a huge garden, you know, and she rattles around in all those rooms. She's on her own, with no family to speak of, so she feels it's pointless hanging on to a house that size. Besides, she's got a friend in Copper Beeches. It's lovely there, more like a hotel than a nursing home.

'Anyway, I told her she shouldn't make any decisions just yet. She should wait till she's feeling better and more like her old self.'

They made a pot of tea and sat companionably at one of the shop tables.

'I fancy a walk on the beach later,' Rachel commented. 'It won't be dark till sevenish so I'll go after we close.'

'Go now if you want to, love. There's nothing happening here and your father will be back in a while. You'll enjoy a bit of fresh air. Not seeing Charlie this evening?' Audrey asked casually.

'No. He called out 'hello' this morning, on his way to look at a sick cow.'

Rachel was careful not to look at her mother as she passed on this last piece of information. Then she brushed back her hair with one hand and stood up.

'OK. If you're sure, I'll go now and take a walk along the beach. Oh, and if it's all right with you, I might go back to London at the weekend to collect the rest of my stuff from the flat. I'll give Dawn a call and see if she'll be around.

She'll be pleased to have all my clobber moved out. I'm not sure where I can put it all once I get it back here, but I suppose there's always the loft.'

'Yes, of course. In fact, I think it's time we had a bit of clear-out of junk from the loft. There may be some hidden treasures up there that we can sell. If we ever get any customers again.'

'Is it quieter than usual this year?'

'A little. Now, get off with you if you're going to the beach, or it will be dark. Are you going to be in for supper?'

'Oh, yes. I'll be back in plenty of time.'

She went to the cottage and dragged out her old waxed jacket. It smelt of sea and sand and horses, and of being stored for too long. She smiled, and pulled on her wellies.

★ ★ ★

It was a half-mile or so walk from the cottage to the sea, along a narrow twisty lane that shelved steeply. It seemed to Rachel that it had been a long time since she'd last walked down there.

As a child, she'd walked along that same lane holding on firmly to one or other of her parents' hands.

As a schoolgirl, she and a crowd of friends had always run down it, anxious to get to the beach to watch the boys and their surfboards.

Then, when she'd become a teenager, she'd carried her own surfboard and competed with her friends for the best waves.

In her later years at school, she'd walked along the lane to the beach shyly holding Charlie's hand, and they'd dawdled home in the dusk, talking of their plans for life and vowing that they'd always be friends.

And although they were still friends, perhaps they had grown too far apart and done too many other things since then to regain that special friendship of first love.

First love. That's what Charlie would

always be for her, despite his comments about them having always been 'mates'.

When she reached the shore, the tide was low, and she walked down to the rocky cove and sniffed the clean air. There was the familiar slight tang of salt — or was it seaweed? — and the gravel scrunched beneath her feet as she reached the water's edge.

She paddled along — and discovered her wellies had a leak. The water squelched into her socks and she pulled a face. She would have blisters by the time she got back up the long lane. She bent to feel the temperature of the water. It was freezing. It would need to warm up a great deal more before she would be venturing into it for a swim.

She sat on a rock and stared at the distant horizon. There was a huge tanker ploughing along, looking as if it was as large as one of the tiny Cornish villages.

'Hello, Little Mermaid,' called a familiar voice.

'Charlie! What are you doing down here?'

'I've been visiting Mrs Eccles. Her dog's not well. She couldn't get it to the surgery so I'm doing a home visit. I thought I'd get a sniff of the sea before I head back to work.'

'Mrs Eccles' old German Shepherd? I can't believe he's still going. What was his name again?'

'Brutus — he must be about fourteen or fifteen now. I'm afraid he won't last much longer, poor thing.'

'That must be so hard — having to tell someone their dog's not going to make it.'

'It is very difficult, especially when you've known the animal all your life. Remember how he used to bark at the gate when we came down to surf? He hated the noise of the surfboards when we ran them down on those old pram wheels. Yes, you're right — it's a tough part of the job.'

'You're probably very good at your job, though.'

He grimaced. '*When* I can convince them I actually know what I'm talking about. I'm so often 'that young lad whose dad's the vet'. But I'm gradually winning them over.'

'Oh, well, I suppose I'd better get back. My wellies have sprung a leak so I shall be squelching all the way up the lane!'

'In that case, allow me to give you a lift. The Range Rover's just back there.'

'Deal! I must say, I was dreading the blisters that I knew would grow from soggy socks! I'll have to get some new wellies now I'm back in the country.'

They walked back to his four-wheel drive and she clambered in. There was a slight smell of antiseptic and the back was full of boxes and tools.

Charlie drove carefully up the narrow lane, ready to stop instantly if anyone came the other way.

'It's the only time of the year I feel I can risk driving down here. In summer it gets so full of holidaymakers who always disbelieve the signs that say limited parking. Well, there you are, madam. At your service. Is Binkie OK?' he asked, remembering what had brought them back together.

'Seems to be. She's still nursing her ears, but the ragged look is definitely improving. Well, thanks again for the lift. See you soon.'

'Are you doing anything at the weekend?' he asked suddenly. 'Only Gemma's coming down and it would be a great chance for you to meet her.'

Rachel's heart sank to her leaky boots. She felt her cheeks colouring and her heart was beating wildly. Thank goodness she wasn't going to be around and so didn't have to make excuses.

'I'm sorry. That would have been lovely, but I'm going back to London to collect my stuff from the flat.'

'That's a pity. Some other time, maybe. I'd like you two to meet.'

'What for? To compare us?' she said without thinking.

'Rachel,' he chided. 'That's not like you. What's that supposed to mean anyway?'

'Nothing. I'm sorry — I said it without thinking. It's been a bit of an emotional time. You know, leaving my job. Moving back here. Meeting you again.'

'Oh, Rachel, Rachel. I'll see you soon. We'll have a drink or something.'

'Maybe. See how the weekend goes. You never know, I might find London is much more attractive after a few days away. I might even decide to stay there after all.'

'I really hope not. I'm pleased we've met up again.'

'Really? But you have Gemma now, don't you? Thanks again for the lift. Have a nice time at the weekend.'

She got out of the car and went quickly up the drive. The shop was closed now, and her parents would be in the kitchen, preparing supper and chatting the way they always did. It was so comforting to find that not quite everything had changed. She took a deep breath and went inside.

'Hi Mum. Dad. I'm back. My wellies have sprung a leak so I'll have to get new ones.'

No Going Back

It seemed the longest drive back to London that Rachel could remember. The city was hectic, and as she arrived back at her flat she knew she had made the right decision in returning to live in Cornwall, even if she had been wavering about her plans.

Her usual parking space was occupied and she drove around looking for somewhere else where she could legally leave her car. It was the usual Friday night problem: people had friends round for drinks or dinner and every slot was taken. Later in the evening, once the visitors had gone, plenty of spaces would be available.

She eventually found a space some distance from her flat and, taking an empty suitcase from her boot, set off towards the place that had been her home for the last four years.

When she arrived, she climbed the stairs and opened the door, conscious that it felt strange to be back, even though she'd only been away for a couple of weeks.

'Hi, Dawn. It's me.'

There was total silence. Dawn must have already gone out for the evening.

Rachel felt deflated and somewhat abandoned. She'd spoken to her flat-mate the previous evening and had said she'd be back by seven-thirty.

Dejectedly she pushed open the door of the sitting-room and suddenly there was a glare of lights and shrieks of 'Surprise!'

A glass was thrust into her hand and she realised that she was surrounded by old friends and workmates, and every-one was cheering and toasting her.

'Wow,' she managed to splutter at last. 'How great to see you all. And thanks, Dawn. I'm really touched that you'd go to all this trouble for me.'

'Well, we couldn't let you leave without a final fling. After all, we might never see you again.'

Rachel felt a lump in her throat. How could she change her mind about leaving now?

After that conversation with Charlie as he'd driven her home from the beach, she'd seriously considering staying in London after all, and had planned to discuss everything carefully with Dawn before she made the final decision. But she could hardly announce at this impromptu going-away party that she wasn't going away after all. She'd look such a fool.

So she'd just have to forget about Charlie and Gemma spending a cosy weekend together and get on with enjoying herself.

'Let's party!' she yelled above the din. Fortunately Dawn had invited all the near neighbours so there shouldn't be any complaints about the noise.

Rachel danced around, greeting people and accepting every offer to refill her glass.

'I think you should have something

to eat,' Dawn suggested tactfully, as her soon-to-be-ex-flatmate became slightly emotional with some of her old colleagues.

'But Des and I go way back! He's missing seeing me in the office each day. He says so. Maybe I should go back and work with him again.'

Des was looking slightly uncomfortable and gratefully handed Rachel over to Dawn's ministrations.

Tucking into a bowl of chilli and rice, she realised how hungry she was. Having planned to take Dawn out for a meal that evening, she'd eaten little more than some fruit and a muesli bar all day. The wine had gone straight to her head and she was grateful to her friend for preventing her from making even more of a fool of herself. As she ate, they stood together in the kitchen.

'What's up, Rachel? Isn't it going quite as planned in Cornwall?'

'It's not that. Remember I told you about Charlie? The schoolgirl's dream? Well, he's back in St Truan working in his father's veterinary practice.'

'Well, that's good, surely?'

'Yes and no. He's still as dishy as ever but he's practically engaged to some high-flying archaeologist.'

'That doesn't sound right. How can an archaeologist be a high-flyer? You can't possibly fly high and dig holes in the ground. Doesn't make sense.'

'She's a university lecturer.'

'Your green-eyed monster is showing. But maybe it will all work out. Hey, you don't mean . . . you're not going to change your mind? Are you? Only I told Karen she could move in on Sunday. She's handed in her notice at her old flat and everything. It would make things very tricky.'

'No, of course I'm not going to change my mind. Don't be silly!'

All thoughts of a heart-to-heart with Dawn had flown out of the window. Rachel had made a commitment and she was going to have to keep to it.

'Come on then. Let's get back to the party!'

'You are OK, aren't you, Rachel?'

'Of course I am. I think I might stick to orange juice for the rest of the evening, though.'

★ ★ ★

After the shop was closed on Saturday evening, Jack and Audrey sat down to have a serious talk. After Rachel had set off for London the previous day, they'd decided they needed to make proper plans for their own future.

'The thing is, we're losing money at an alarming rate. Well, losing it might not be quite the way to put it, but we're certainly spending it without replenishing it,' Jack began.

'And if we go on at this rate, we might not be able to sell the shop as a going concern,' added Audrey.

'But I reckon a property developer might look at it with an eye to profit.'

'So, if we sell the house and the shop, will we have enough money to buy somewhere else and still have enough left over to live on?'

'Only if we sell both properties for a really good price. I mean, I won't get a pension for another few years and, as you say, we still have to have something to live on. But in any case, we can hardly sell either the shop or the cottage while Rachel needs our support. If we did buy another place, we'd have to make sure she had at least a room of her own.'

'My lovely labour-saving bungalow with no stairs . . . all a bit of a dream now, isn't it? So, we're back to selling off some of our own antiques for now, just to give us a bit of income. We should make a list of the things we don't really need and get that auctioneer from Truro to give us an estimate. There's that huge great bureau for starters. I'd be glad to see the back of that. All that carving takes an age to dust. And it's only got old rubbish in it — papers and stuff we don't need to keep any more.'

'And that pair of Edwardian chairs in

the hall. They're painted rosewood, very desirable at the moment and probably worth at least a thousand for the two. They're in really good condition.'

'Really? That much? I've always liked them, though.'

'So have I, but we never use them for fear of damaging them. It's things like that that we should be considering letting go.'

'You're right. And if we ever do get our bungalow, there wouldn't be room for them anyway. A few thousand pounds here and there will help for now. I'm just not sure what we'll say to Rachel to explain why we're selling off our own possessions. I really don't want her to think that we're on our uppers or that she's in the way here.'

'Well, let's call the auctioneer on Monday and see what he says.'

Feeling a little happier, they settled down to watch their favourite TV quiz game.

★　★　★

Rachel drove back to Cornwall on Sunday morning. As she set off, the streets around the London flat were quiet, and the hustle of weekday traffic seemed a million miles away. With mixed emotions she wondered if she would ever return to live in that city again, or ever visit the many friends with whom she had promised to keep in touch.

She'd handed out loads of the Cranhams' Curios business cards that she'd printed, and all her friends had promised to look at the website and some had even said they'd put in bids on her auctions, if only to bump up the prices. All perfectly legal, they had assured her. But they didn't want to be lumbered with paying out for things they didn't want, so it was unlikely ever to happen.

Soon she was out on the motorway and speeding along at seventy. Her little car was running well, despite being packed to the roof with all her belongings from her years in London.

She'd left lots of stuff behind in the flat for Dawn and her new flatmate to use. She hardly needed things such as spare kettles and toasters while she was living with her parents, and if and when she moved out, well, she'd simply have to buy new ones.

She fingered the necklace her friends had given her. They'd clubbed together and bought her a piece of modern designer jewellery from one of the little shops near the flat. She was very touched at their thoughtfulness and knew she would treasure it always.

It was afternoon by the time she reached Exeter. The roads had been busy all the way on the journey and she'd been held up several times. But once she got beyond Exeter, the A30 opened up in front of her and she could speed up again. Already the air seemed clearer and the light more intense.

An hour later and she was well into her beloved Cornwall. She pulled into a lay-by and took her mobile from her bag to phone her mother.

'Hi, Mum. I'm about half an hour away. I hope you've got the roast on — I'm starving!'

'No roast today, I'm afraid, sweetheart. I'm doing a casserole instead. I thought it wouldn't matter then what time you got back. Had a good time, love?'

'Great, thanks. They'd organised a party for me when I got back on Friday night. I spent yesterday getting over it! See you soon.'

Rachel wondered if Charlie's Gemma was driving in the opposite direction on her way back to Bristol. She realised now that any dreams she may have had of a future with him were impossible and, sensibly, she should refuse any further invitations to go out with him.

But she knew she probably wouldn't be sensible. Besides, she was curious to know how Gemma's weekend visit had gone. Nastily, she half-hoped it hadn't gone at all well!

She stopped outside the cottage and

began to unload her things.

'Hi, folks! I'm here. I've got tons of stuff to unload. Are you going to help me, Dad? Can you carry some of it straight up to my room? I'll have to live in a tip for a few days till I can sort it out. Maybe a personal jumble sale will be the answer!'

'Leave it in the hall and I'll start carrying things upstairs.'

'Thanks, Dad. I might have to leave some of it in the car for now though. It's starting to rain.'

★   ★   ★

'Whatever did we do before black sacks?' Rachel asked, brandishing the tenth black binbag that she'd brought in from the car.

'We had suitcases and owned much less stuff,' her mother commented. 'When I was your age, I had two going-out dresses and the rest was carefully mended to last.'

'And dinosaurs roamed the beaches

and ten of us shared a slice of bread on Saturdays, if we were lucky,' Rachel mocked fondly, and despite herself, her mother laughed.

'Oh, it's so nice to be back!' Rachel drew both her parents into a hug. 'Thanks for being here for me.'

Her parents smiled and exchanged glances. Maybe it *was* the right thing to have Rachel back at home, even if it did mean a few plans had to be changed or postponed.

'Come on then. Let's have something to eat.'

After supper, they all sat together watching one of the natural history programmes that seemed to have become traditional TV fare for Sunday evenings.

But by ten o'clock, Rachel was falling asleep. She made her excuses and went up to bed, except that her bed was covered in black sacks and she couldn't get into it. She muttered beneath her breath and piled up the sacks beneath the window, with a promise to herself that she would sort them out the next day.

Then she saw her laptop on the chest of drawers and realised her auction would be finishing very soon. She hadn't even checked on its progress. Tired though she was, she couldn't resist the temptation to look, and switched the machine on to warm up while she went to brush her teeth.

When she came back from the bathroom, she clicked away until she found the auction site and her face split into a broad grin. Her mother had priced the Beswick horse at eighteen pounds in the shop, and she knew Audrey would always offer a discount on top of that. Now the bidding for it on the Internet site stood at thirty-nine pounds and there were still people bidding with twenty minutes to go.

She went to her bedroom door and called down to her parents.

'The auction's ending. I don't know

if you'd like to watch what's happening?'

Her father came upstairs and stood behind her, looking at the computer screen.

'What's going on now?' he asked.

'Well, the organisers set a time for the auction to end and whoever gets the last bid in, buys the item. And the last time I looked, the bidding was standing at forty-one pounds.'

She pressed a button and the screen changed and a new price came up.

'Somebody really wants this horse,' she said excitedly, as the price rose to forty-eight.

Then it was all over with the top bid standing at forty-eight pounds.

'But we have to post the horse to the buyer. That will cut the profits.'

'Not at all. The postage is charged separately. Tell Mum her eighteen-pound horse has made a nice profit — thirty pounds more than she was asking for it in the shop.'

'I'm still not sure if I understand how

it works, but if you say it's right, then I'm sure it is.'

'There are other things of ours up for sale on the site but I need to find my bed for now and we can look again in the morning. Night, Dad.'

She slept soundly, exhausted by her long drive and the hectic weekend.

★ ★ ★

The next morning, Rachel had to find room for all the belongings that she'd brought back with her from London. Fortunately the wardrobe had plenty of space.

After breakfast, she checked on the auction site again, and although nothing else had made quite as much profit as the horse, she'd still managed to make over two hundred pounds in total.

Once the money arrived, she would post off the goods.

Her parents were enthusiastic about her auctioneering efforts and were already looking out more items for her to sell.

Feeling pleased with her success and their support, she went back to her precious laptop and put the finishing touches to her website, planning to give her parents a demonstration of how it worked after they'd closed the shop for the day.

Then she placed bids on a couple of collections of small pieces of pottery, knowing that if she got them at a bargain price, she could sell them again at a profit.

She'd just finished doing all this and had switched off her machine when she heard the door open downstairs. On her way down to the hall, she saw her mother come in accompanied by a tall man carrying a clipboard.

'Hello. What's going on?'

'Just pop over to help your father in the shop, will you, love?' said her mother, who obviously had no intention of making any introductions.

Scowling slightly, Rachel went over to the shop.

'Dad? Who's that? In the cottage, with Mum?'

'If you must know, he's the auctioneer from Truro. We're going to get rid of a few of our larger pieces of furniture. It's pointless keeping stuff we don't really want, and trying to keep everything clean is getting your mother down.'

'I see. Selling off the family heirlooms, eh? Times must be harder than I realised.' She paused and stared at her father. 'Dad, times *are* harder than I realised, aren't they?'

'Well, we haven't been making much lately. In fact, it's costing us more to keep the shop open than we're making from it.'

'But why are things so bad?'

'I think it's just that there's not so much money about, and the competition from the new place isn't going to help. There's a new craft centre opening about a mile from St Truan. They've only opened part of it so far, but once they get going, I understand they're planning to do antiques, a snack bar and various craft displays.'

'What? How did they get permission for something like that? Have you been to check it out?'

'Of course not. Everyone knows me round here. They'd know exactly why I was there and probably boot me out.'

'Then I'll go. I need to go out to buy some new wellies anyhow. I'll call in there on my way. What a cheek! So, what exactly do you plan to sell from the house?'

'We thought that pair of Edwardian chairs in the hall and the old monstrosity of a bureau. It's as much to clear space as anything, and to give your mother a few things less to dust.'

'But we've always had those chairs.'

'Exactly, and how many times have you ever sat on them?'

'Only the once as I remember. You nearly skinned me alive and said they weren't chairs for sitting on, just to look at. OK, so I get the point. What are they worth?'

'Possibly a thousand?'

'Wow. That's more than I thought. Well, I'm going wellie shopping now, if that's all right with you. And I'll go on a spying mission, too. Why didn't you tell me about this new craft-cum-antiques centre before?'

'We've had a lot to talk about since you got back. Go on then or it'll be closing time before you even start out.'

* * *

Rachel drove out of the village on the road her father had directed her to take, and she soon arrived at the once derelict barns that had been converted into a large retail outlet with masses of car parking space.

That was one up to them, for a start. The only way anyone could get to Cranhams' Curios was to walk from the village car park. Fortunately, many people stopped in the picturesque little village to look around, and the shop was conveniently placed to offer a break in their wanderings. All the same, having this new craft-cum-antiques centre opening up so close to them was very worrying.

Only one of the shops was actually open but she could peer in through the windows of the others to see what they were planning to sell. There was a candle shop . . . no problem there. A fudge shop . . . again, no competition. The third shop she came to had a large sign outside:

'Antiques and Curios . . . today's treasures, antiques of tomorrow. Objets d'art bought and sold.'

This was serious competition. She looked through the window at what was on offer. There were one or two nice looking pieces and a whole lot of items that were clearly copies or fakes. It looked as if someone's granny had cleared out their china cabinet and that this formed the main basis of the smaller items of their stock.

She walked away and saw the café

was open and went inside for a cup of tea. It was served in quite a nice mug but it came from a large pot that had obviously been standing for some time and it tasted stewed.

At least that was one good point in Cranhams' Curios' favour. Fresh tea was made for every customer and served in small, individual teapots. But as she sat, she could see this place was going to be a big problem for her parents. This was almost certainly one of the reasons for their trade falling off, even if it wasn't yet fully open.

Deep in thought, she drove on to the next town to buy her new wellington boots. Who was behind the new enterprise? Probably someone from upcountry with more money than they knew what to do with. It was all very worrying.

★　★　★

After supper that evening, Rachel brought her laptop downstairs and set it up in the living-room.

'Right, you two, I want to show you what I've done. I'll need to plug it in to the phone for a little while, but if anyone tries to ring, they'll get the engaged tone and they can call back later. Watch carefully now.'

When the main menu came up, she ordered her father to type in *www.cranhams-curios.com*. He did this and watched as the photo that Rachel had taken of himself and Audrey outside the shop came up on the screen.

'Well, now, will you look at that?' he said. 'Audrey! Just look! Isn't our girl clever? It's a lovely picture of you, dear.'

'And doesn't the shop look nice! Oh, and the village!'

Rachel beamed with pleasure. So far so good.

'Now click on the door of the shop. Here — move the mouse.'

She showed her father how to make the arrow move around the screen. She pressed the button and the door opened. Once inside, the pictures moved along to show the various displays of items for sale, and then went into the little kitchen area where a picture appeared of Audrey with a plate piled high with her home-made scones. Then there was a series of close-ups of the best of their porcelain figurines and other small nick-nacks. Right at the end was a message: *Thank you for visiting our website. We hope to welcome you in person when you next visit our beautiful country of Cornwall.*

'So, what do you think?' Rachel asked.

'It's wonderful, love,' said Audrey. 'But I'm not sure how this will improve our trade. I mean to say, this is all just on your computer.'

'But it will be on everyone's computer. Everyone who types in our web address.'

'The www thing?'

Rachel nodded. 'It may do no good at all, but it's worth a try. Tell you what, if we type in the address from one of the adverts you were showing me, you'll see what I mean.'

She picked up her mother's magazine and typed in the web address of one of the advertisers. Immediately, pictures of a skirt and blouse appeared on the screen, and an order form.

'See, if you click here and here, the item is ordered.'

'But I don't really want it.'

'Don't worry, Mum. We haven't put in our postal address or paid for it. I just click this little cross at the top of the page and whoosh ... it all disappears. Easy, isn't it?'

'If you say so.'

'Just trust me, Mum. I'll look after it all.'

She unplugged the machine from the phone line and switched it off.

Within a few minutes, the phone rang. Audrey answered at once, anxious in case it was her friend, Marjorie, trying to contact her.

'It's Charlie, for you,' she said, handing the phone to her daughter. 'We'll go and put the kettle on. Leave you in peace. Come on, Jack.'

Rachel smiled at their tactfulness.

Audrey Takes A Tumble

'Hi, Rachel! So, you did come back. I wondered if you might change your mind.'

'I thought about it, Charlie, but I know Cornwall is the right place for me. Besides, I've bought some new wellies and I know I'd never wear them in London.'

'You're right. A serious investment like that — you need to get your money's worth from them.'

'So, did you have a good weekend?'

'Great, thanks. We didn't really do much but it was nice to have Gemma around.'

'Good. I enjoyed myself, too. Dawn, my now ex-flatmate, had organised a surprise party for me so I caught up with lots of old friends and colleagues.'

'I was wondering if we could talk?'

'Isn't that what we're doing now?'

'You know what I mean. Meet up and talk.'

'Oh, well . . . ' Rachel was hesitant. Perhaps he and Gemma had got properly engaged and that was what he wanted to tell her. Or maybe it was the opposite and they had split up?

'Please, Rachel. The last time we met, you seemed to be annoyed with me for some reason. We need to clear the air between us. Let's have a meal out tomorrow night.'

'All right,' she agreed, knowing this had the potential to be the worst date of her life.

'Pick you up at seven-thirty?'

'OK. I'll be ready and waiting. Thanks. 'Bye, Charlie.'

She put down the phone and thought about his words. It did sound as if he was warning her off. Why else would he want to 'clear the air'? She felt depressed but knew that if she let her parents see it, they would worry, and they had worries enough as it was.

She pulled herself together and went

into the kitchen.

She breezed in as brightly as possible and tried to sound enthusiastic about the next evening.

'But something's not quite right, is it, love?' her perceptive father asked.

'Oh, I don't know. I think he's got some news after his weekend with Gemma. He made comments about us needing to clear the air.'

'Don't worry about it. What will be will be and all that. Just try to enjoy yourself.'

'Of course I will. Now, where's this coffee?'

⋆　⋆　⋆

The following day seemed endless and Rachel's thoughts were seldom far from Charlie and what he might have to tell her that evening. She tried several times to convince herself that she was being ridiculous — that she simply had a crush on him just as she'd had in her schooldays. She was twenty-six, for goodness sake and should know better.

All the same, she dressed carefully for her evening out, casual but smart. She had washed her hair and brushed it so it shone, and she left it hanging loose.

'You look lovely, dear,' her mother encouraged her. 'That shade really suits you. I hope you have a good time.'

'Thanks, Mum. Oh, there's Charlie's Range Rover now. I'll see you later.'

Charlie's vehicle was always crammed with an assortment of vet's paraphernalia but that night there seemed to be even more equipment squeezed into it than usual.

'Sorry about the mobile surgery. I'm afraid I'm on call. I'd hoped Dad would take over from me this evening but he'd already arranged to go out. I just hope nobody bothers us. We don't get called out all that often so I thought we might as well risk it and go ahead with our plans.'

'Fine. So, where are we going?'

'To a little place out at Poltor. It's quiet there and the mobile gets reception if I'm needed. There are an awful lot of black spots in Cornwall for phone reception. Especially down in the little coves.'

They drove along almost in silence, Rachel having decided to let Charlie lead the conversation.

The pub had only one other couple in the restaurant area.

Charlie and Rachel chose their food, then sat back.

'So, what do you want to talk about?' she asked, after a long pause.

'Well, us really. I wanted to be sure there were no misunderstandings.'

'Why would there be? Has something happened with Gemma?'

'Nothing in particular. I did mention that we'd been seeing each other, you and I, but she was quite all right about it. She understands that we've been friends since school days.'

'But we're not the same two people that we were back then,' put in Rachel. 'Everyone changes as they experience life. I know we have similar backgrounds and therefore a lot in common, but you've had years away, training to be a vet. I've had several years of working in London and enjoying a more city sort of existence. I'd like to get to know the current version of Charlie much better — so long as Gemma is OK with that?'

'Oh, I'm sure she is. Here's to friendship.'

He raised his mineral water and they touched glasses.

The evening passed pleasantly as the two young people chatted amiably and they were about to order pudding when Charlie's mobile rang.

'I need to take this. Excuse me.'

He became very professional as he spoke on the phone, glancing at his watch now and again.

'OK. I'll get there as soon as I can. It may be a little while, though. I'm not actually at home and I have to drop someone off first.'

He ended the call and apologised to Rachel for the interruption.

'I'm sorry about this but it's an

emergency, I'm afraid — a cow with a difficult birth.'

'There's no need for you to take me home. I can get a taxi,' she offered. 'Or I could come with you if it'd help. I'd quite like that.'

'Well, if you wouldn't mind. That would save me lots of time, but you're hardly dressed for a cowshed. I think there may be an overall in the back of the car, and probably some spare — but rather giant — wellies.'

'Sounds good to me. I'd be interested to see you at work.'

He paid the bill and they went out to his Range Rover.

'Will the cow be all right?'

'I hope so. She's a good milker so they won't want to lose her.'

'So you'd save the cow at the expense of the calf, if necessary?'

'Probably. But chances are we can save them both. It's just down this lane. Hang on tight. It gets pretty bumpy.'

'Heavens. No wonder you need a four-wheel drive.'

They stopped in the farmyard and Charlie went to the back of the Range Rover and pulled out two sets of overalls and some boots.

'Bit smelly, I'm afraid, but at least they'll cover you up.'

'Me and several others, I guess!'

She used her belt to haul up the long overalls and to pull them in at the waist. By keeping her shoes on inside the boots, they fitted reasonably well. Fortunately she'd worn flat heels.

They went into the barn where the farmer was waiting. It smelled of warm hay and animals. Not an unpleasant smell at all, she thought.

'Let's have a look. Wait over there, Rachel, just in case she lashes out. Come on, old girl. Let's see what's the problem . . .'

Charlie rolled up his sleeves and dipped his arms into a bucket of soapy water, scrubbing them as he did so.

'I'm going to need ropes,' he muttered.

'There are some here. I thought you

might need them. Got the calf's legs all folded back, hasn't she?' said the farmer.

'Looks like it.'

The two men worked together and Rachel watched, forgetting her squeamishness in her anxiety for the poor cow, who mooed pitifully throughout the whole procedure.

It was amazing. Somehow, the ropes were looped over the calf's feet and both of the men tugged, just at the moment the cow had a contraction. The little calf flopped wetly down on to the straw and lay there quivering. Its mother mooed even more loudly and bent down to lick her baby, and within a very short time, the calf stood on spindly legs and wobbled around until it found its mother's teat. Rachel felt almost moved to tears.

'Nice little heifer you've got there.'

'Thanks, Charlie. I'm delighted. If she's half as good as her mother at milking, it's been a good night's work. Now, if you'll come back into the farmhouse, the two of you, I'll get you a drop of something to warm you up.'

'Thanks, but we'd better get back.'

'Oh, I'm sorry. I spoilt your evening out, didn't I?'

'This is Rachel Cranham, by the way.'

'How do you do, my dear. You must be Jack's daughter?'

'Yes, that's right.'

'I used to play cricket with your dad, way back. Give him my regards. We'll have to have a drink together one evening.'

★　★　★

As Charlie drove Rachel home, she told him how impressed she'd been as she'd watched him work.

'It was all most interesting. I enjoyed it.'

'What, smells and all?' He laughed. 'And you all nicely dressed up for a quiet meal out. That's the problem with going out with a vet. You have to take me muck and all.'

She wondered about his use of the expression 'going out with'.

'I'm sorry it's so late,' he went on. 'Oh! I hope your parents aren't waiting up for you. Look, there are lights on everywhere in the cottage.'

'They don't usually wait up. They seem to have grasped the fact that I'm a big girl now.'

'All the same, I'd like to make sure all's well. I'll see you to the door.'

He switched off the engine and accompanied her up the drive. The door opened as they approached and her father stood there, looking white-faced.

'Dad? Whatever's wrong?'

'It's your mum — she took a tumble. She won't let me call a doctor. She says our own doctor won't come at night and she doesn't want anyone else. Sorry, Charlie! Hello to you, son.'

'Hello. Where's Mrs Cranham now?'

'Sitting on the sofa. She was halfway up the stairs and lost her footing. It was easier to get her down than up.'

'Shall I take a look?' offered Charlie. 'I know I'm a vet but animals and humans have a lot in common. I might be able to advise.'

'Thanks — I'd be most grateful.'

They all trooped into the living-room where Audrey was sitting with a blanket over her, looking very pale.

'Mum, what on earth have you been doing?'

'Sorry. It was so silly. I don't know what happened.'

'Let me have a look,' Charlie offered. 'I can probably tell if any bones are broken.'

He moved the blanket and felt carefully along Audrey's shin, which was where she said it hurt. Although there was a bruise and a lump on her leg, he didn't think it was broken.

'But I think you should get it X-rayed to be sure. Keep it still for now and we'll put a cold compress on it to bring down that swelling. Have you got any frozen peas?'

'I don't use frozen vegetables.' Audrey sniffed. 'But there's one of those polythene wine chiller things. Rachel bought it for us last Christmas.'

'Perfect,' Charlie announced. 'Get it for me, will you, Rachel, and bring a towel to wrap it in? We don't want to add to the problem with freezer burn. Now, keep yourself warm and don't try to move, Mrs Cranham. And I think you should call the doctor in the morning. I don't want you to get into trouble for seeing the vet instead of your GP.'

'Thanks so much, Charlie. You're a good lad.'

'No problem. How did it happen?'

'On that dark corner of those stairs of ours. It turns round, and somehow I just didn't see where I was putting my feet.'

'Rachel mentioned that you may have a cataract? Have you had anyone check it out? Cataracts are often a problem in dim light. They upset your ability to focus. You should get your eyes checked while you're at the doctor's about your ankle. It's such an easy operation these days. In and out in the same day. Think about it. Next time, a fall could be so much more serious. Now, I must go. I have an early start — in about four hours to be precise.'

Rachel saw him out, thanking him again, and he promised to call round to see her mum the next day.

'Why didn't you phone my mobile to let me know what had happened, Dad?' she asked as she came back in from the hall.

'I didn't like to interrupt your evening.'

'Thanks, but it really wouldn't have mattered. By the way, we ended up at a farm, talking to someone who knows you. Somebody Perry? He said you used to play cricket together.'

'Goodness, what were you doing on a farm at midnight?'

'Helping deliver a calf. It was amazing.'

'Good grief. Did you hear that,

Audrey? Our little city girl's turning into a vet's assistant.'

'You'd better get some rest,' was Audrey's answer. 'I'll be fine here. Go on, the two of you. You'll have to manage without me in the morning.'

Rachel and her father went up the narrow stairs. Perhaps now, her mum would agree to let someone look at her eyes. As long as there wasn't much else wrong, it might make her see reason and get herself sorted out.

Once she was lying in bed, Rachel reflected on the evening. She felt quite wide awake but needed to get some sleep so that she'd be alert enough to manage the shop in the morning.

As she finally drifted off, she remembered what Charlie had said as they'd driven away from Mr Perry's farm — 'That's the problem with going out with a vet. You have to take me muck and all.'

* * *

Jack drove Audrey round to the doctor's as soon as he could get an appointment for her.

'Shall I come in with you, love?' he asked.

'I think you might have to. I don't think I'll be able to walk into the surgery without help.'

When her name was called, he helped her along the corridor and opened the door to Dr Graham's consulting room. The doctor had known them for many years and helped Audrey to a seat.

'What on earth have you been doing? Let's have a look.'

He removed the bandage and peered at her injury.

'This doesn't look too bad. I expect it's been pretty painful but there isn't much swelling.'

He felt along the bone, just as Charlie had done, and agreed that he didn't think anything was broken.

'I could send you for an X-ray, just to be sure, but I'm fairly confident that it's just bruised.'

'If it is broken, what would they do?'

'Nothing much. It would probably be a crack in the shin bone and you'd just need to take it easy. I think you did exactly the right thing with it.'

'That was Charlie's advice. He put a cold pack on it and that seemed to take down the swelling. You know Charlie Williams, of course. The young vet? I think I'll probably not bother with an X-ray. Thank you, though.'

The doctor nodded.

To Jack's surprise, Audrey continued, 'Now, I'd like you to take a look at my eyes, please. I think I may have a cataract. In fact that's probably why I fell. It was a bit dark on the corner of the stairs and I couldn't see properly.'

'OK. Let's take a look . . . Oh, yes. This is a nasty one. It needs attention as fast as we can get you looked at. I'd say it's been developing over quite a few months. It's only the one eye that's really bad. The other is fine for the time being, though it may develop problems at some point. I expect you've been managing quite well with one eye and putting off getting it seen to?'

Audrey had the grace to blush. 'Well, maybe just a bit. I didn't want to be out of action, you see. Jack can't manage on his own, but now Rachel's back home for a while, it's more convenient to have it looked at.'

The doctor wrote out a letter for her to take to the eye specialist at the local hospital and phoned to make an appointment for her, stressing the urgency.

'They'll send you an appointment as soon as they can. When they do, take this letter with you. You shouldn't have to wait for too long under the circumstances.'

'Thanks. And I hope you're right that it won't take long for me to get over it. I can't do with being laid up.'

Rachel was delighted to hear the news. In fact, everything seemed to be going well that day.

While her parents had been away visiting the doctor, there had been a couple of customers in the shop, one of whom had made an offer on a nice old mahogany desk. His offer wasn't for quite as much as Rachel thought the desk was worth, but after considerable haggling, they had reached a compromise, and the customer was coming back the following morning with the money and to collect his purchase.

* * *

Over the next weeks, as spring arrived, the tourists began to arrive, too. Daffodils bloomed along the sides of the roads, trees came into leaf and the whole county seemed fresh and green, as if it had been thoroughly washed after the winter. And Rachel and Charlie got into the habit of going out together two or three nights each week, much as they had done when they'd been 'mates' during their schooldays.

Rachel had managed the shop most days whilst her mother's leg was recovering, and Audrey had been to visit the eye specialist at the local hospital. Now that she was on the list for treatment, she seemed to have come to terms with the idea.

At last the day of the operation arrived, and Jack drove Audrey to the hospital.

She was to telephone when she was ready for him to collect her afterwards.

Rachel stayed in the shop and made scones to serve with the coffees and teas, just as her mother always did. She knew that her baking was almost as good as her mum's, and was pleased that she was here when she was needed.

She made a few more sales on her auction site as well.

She was in the middle of changing the window display when the phone rang.

'Rachel? It's Marjorie. Is your mother there?'

'No. She's having her cataract done today. Is there anything wrong?'

'Not really. I'm sorry, I'd forgotten it was today. Give her my love, will you?

Tell her I've got some news and I want to talk to her when she's better.'

'OK. I hope everything's all right.'

'I'll tell you when I see you. Perhaps you and your mother will come round for tea when she's better? I have a few things to discuss with her . . . with you both, actually.'

'Now you *have* got me intrigued.'

'Nothing to worry about. Goodbye, dear.'

Rachel frowned. She hoped Marjorie's news wasn't something that would upset her mother. Especially not at this time. Audrey was stressed enough as it was. Or so she thought.

'Your mum's as happy as Larry,' Jack told Rachel when he came back from the hospital. 'She was organising everyone and telling the other patients not to worry — that the operation was nothing and that it would all be over in no time.'

'Typical. Good old Mum. Do you know what's going on with Auntie Marjorie? Only she wants Mum and me to go round to see her. Says she's got some news and something to discuss with us both.'

'Haven't a clue. Don't tell your mother today though or she'll only start worrying.'

By the time she returned home in the evening, Audrey was an expert on cataracts and their treatment.

'I really don't know why I put it off for so long. Nothing to it. My eye's a bit weepy but that's to be expected, isn't it? Now, has anyone done anything about supper? I'm starving.'

Just Good Friends

One morning, about a week after the operation, Audrey came back over to the cottage from the shop in a fury.

'Just look at this.' She waved a printed sheet of bright yellow paper in Rachel's face. 'The cheek of it! Honestly, fancy putting it through *our* door.'

'Steady on, Mum. What on earth is it?'

'That dratted craft and antiques centre. They're having a grand opening and we're 'cordially invited to go along and buy something from their amazing selection of bargains'. I can't believe they would do such a thing. Putting one through our door of all places.'

'I expect they've paid somebody to put one through every door and it was nothing personal.'

'Hmm. Maybe. But I wouldn't go there if they were *giving* stuff away. I expect it's all a load of junk anyhow.'

'I might go and take another look. When is this grand opening?'

'Tomorrow.'

'OK. And how about us going to see Auntie Marjorie later today? She said she wants to see us both and I'm sure Dad's coping all right.'

★ ★ ★

'Come in, my dears. Lovely to see you,' said Marjorie when they arrived at her house.

They made small talk for a few minutes and Rachel was beginning to feel slightly impatient.

'So, what's this news you've got for us that's such a big secret?' she asked bluntly.

'I've put the house on the market and I've got a place at the Copper Beeches. I'm moving in as soon as the house is sold, or maybe even before. I think I shall love it there. It's such a welcoming atmosphere.'

'Oh, Marjorie, dear, are you sure?' Audrey was shocked.

'Quite certain. I don't want to have to look after this big old place any more. I want to enjoy life and be waited on a bit. Now, what I wanted to say to you and Rachel is this: I want you to take all my old clutter and either sell it in your shop or send it to the auction rooms. I don't want anything for it — I just want to see the back of it. Of course, if there's anything you want to keep yourselves, that's up to you. All I shall be taking with me is my collection of figurines and one or two pieces of my mother's silver. The rest is going to a good home . . . namely, yours.'

'But, Marjorie, there's so much of it.'

'And some of it must be very valuable,' Rachel couldn't stop herself from adding.

'Really? That's lovely for you then. Once I've decided exactly what to keep for myself, I'd like you to come round and clear out the rest for me. Will you do that?'

'But you can't just give it all away. I mean . . . '

'If I can't let my oldest friend have it, who can I give it all to? I couldn't bear to sell it myself and I don't have any close family to speak of. Anyway, I intend to have a good many more years in the Copper Beeches with just a few selected pieces to keep me company. I don't know why I've hung on to it all for so long. I hope you'll both come and visit me there?'

* * *

They explained it all to Jack when they got back home.

'I can hardly believe it,' Rachel burbled. 'There's stuff there that must be worth hundreds. You don't think she's gone . . . well, a bit strange?'

'Not at all,' said Audrey. 'She's very well off. The house will fetch a packet and she's got plenty put by. Her husband left her a sizeable amount, so I shouldn't worry too much. They never had children.'

'This could really make a difference to us.' Rachel was excited. 'Perhaps we could even do a bit of modernisation in the shop on the proceeds?'

'Whoa, steady on. We haven't sold any of Marjorie's bits and pieces yet. Now, didn't you say you and Charlie are going out this evening?'

Her mother began to sort out their evening meal and Rachel went to change, her mind still buzzing.

★ ★ ★

'I could hardly believe it,' she told Charlie when they were settled in the pub. 'All those lovely things and we're going to have them in our shop. Real quality stuff. That'll teach those upstarts at the so-called craft and antiques centre. I mean to say, have you seen some of the rubbish they're calling antiques? I'm going round tomorrow to their grand opening. I think it's so unfair, opening a huge place like that so near our lovely village. Don't you think so?'

'Are you going to have something to eat?' he asked. 'I'm having the pasta and mushrooms.'

'Same for me, please. But, honestly, the aggressive marketing they're doing! Can you believe they put one of their flyers through our shop door? *Our* shop door. The direct competition.'

'I'll go and order.'

When he came back she continued her tirade about the new shops. But Charlie didn't want to talk about the problems of Cranhams' Curios.

'Please,' he said after a while. 'Can't we talk about something else? I know you're upset and excited at the same time, but I don't think there's anything I can usefully say on the subject.'

'Well, I'm sorry if I'm boring you. Maybe you'd rather talk about sick animals. How many cows have you cured today?'

'Sorry, but I . . . well, I just wanted to relax. Come on, tell me about your plans then.'

'Not if you're not interested.'

'It isn't that.'

The evening wasn't a great success and several times Rachel had the feeling that Charlie was about to tell her something he thought was important, only for him to change his mind and either clam up or change the subject.

She wondered if he was beginning to realise that she wanted to be more than just 'mates,' and how difficult it was for her, knowing that Gemma was always in the background.

It was almost reaching the point where she needed to decide one way or the other — should she continue to see Charlie or not?

* * *

Rachel couldn't persuade her mother to accompany her to the opening of the new centre and so she went along on her own.

It was quite an impressive set-up, she had to admit. All the units were open by now and were filled with the sort of presents that tourists like to take home.

There was also a lot of rubbish, she thought. A lot of tacky gifts amongst a few better items. There were also several stands of reproduction antiques — copper kettles and model buildings made of plastic — which she hated.

All the same, the centre was going to be quite a draw, and would undoubtedly take away from their own business. She promised herself that she would make frequent visits to check out how they were doing and what they had on sale. She still had no idea who owned the place or how it had been financed.

She reported all this back to her parents, who seemed most concerned at the potential threat to their own trade.

They also seemed determined that, because Rachel had been spending so much time looking after the shop and cottage, she should have a day off to go shopping in Truro.

So she drove to Truro and wandered round the shops, not really wanting anything in particular and with no reason to buy anything other than for the sake of it.

'Rachel Cranham! I don't believe it! What are you doing here?'

'Chloe! How great to see you! You're looking wonderful.'

'All due to the love of a good man.'

Rachel's old friend held out her left hand to show Rachel a sparkling diamond ring.

'Wow! Who's the lucky guy? And what are you doing back in Cornwall? The last I heard, you were working overseas on an aid project.'

'Yes, in Malaysia. Amazing place. But that's all in the past. Let's grab a coffee. I'm exhausted. We'll go in here.'

They somehow managed to order coffee in between Chloe's excited outpourings. She hadn't changed so much, her friend realised.

'Anyway, I've been living at my brother Dan's place since I came back to the UK. Dan and his wife, Jayne, have a B and B called Sea Haven. But

Mike and I will be getting married in two weeks' time. Oh, Mike's an architect . . . or nearly. He's finishing his university course but works for his father. Well, actually, he's more or less taken over from his father. We're converting a barn at Dan's place so we'll be living there.'

'Chloe, could you slow down a bit! I think I got lost on the second sentence. At least I've gathered you're getting married soon and his name's Mike.'

'Yes. Mike Polglaze. Good old Cornish stock. Hey, you must come to the wedding! You're going to be around for the next couple of weeks?'

'Oh, yes, I'll be around indefinitely. I'm back living at home, for now.'

'Great! I'll get Jayne to send you an invitation. She's organising everything. There's a lot of the old crowd coming. It'll be wonderful.'

Half an hour later, Rachel felt exhausted. Chloe had always been one for showing great enthusiasm and clearly she was no different now.

'I'll have to go, Rachel. I've still got heaps to do. We'll catch up properly after the wedding. Well, obviously I'll see you *at* the wedding, but I don't suppose we'll have a lot of time to gossip. Bring someone with you if you like. I'll get Jayne to send the invitation for you and a guest.'

'Thanks. It's lovely to see you so happy.'

Rachel continued her shopping, thinking that now she had a good excuse to buy something new to wear. She wondered if she could ask Charlie to go with her to Chloe's wedding. After all, he had known Chloe too, from schooldays.

She trailed around the shops for most of the morning, finally deciding on a simple short-sleeved fitted jacket and long flowing skirt in delicate shades of blue and turquoise. Sea colours, she thought. The top was a deeper shade of turquoise and she added a soft scarf to complete the outfit. Pleased with herself, she drove home.

'Guess who I met?' she asked, bursting into the shop and dropping her bags all over the floor.

She poured out her news and showed her mother her new purchases.

'Fancy! Little Chloe getting married.'

'Little Chloe? She's the same age as me!'

'Well, yes, I suppose she is, but she always seemed much younger. Such a bouncy little thing.'

'No change there. Honestly, I could hardly get a word in. I'll take this lot over to the house and get something to eat. I'm starving. Great to see her though, and to see her so happy.'

★ ★ ★

A couple of days later, the wedding invitation arrived. 'Must be costing someone a fortune,' Rachel commented, noticing that it was taking place at one of the swankiest local hotels. 'That place is expensive even for drinks. I thought I might ask

Charlie to go with me.'

'That would be nice. By the way, do you think you might take Binkie to see him again? Her ears are looking a bit inflamed again. They'd cleared up nicely but now the infection seems to have come back. You can ask him about the wedding at the same time.'

Rachel took the cat along to the surgery later that day. The waiting-room was busy but she settled down with a magazine and flicked through it until at last her turn came.

'Hi. You should have told the receptionist you're a friend of mine. I would have seen you earlier.'

'Can't expect any special favours,' she said with a grin. 'How are you doing?'

'Fine. Sorry I haven't been in touch for a while. Busy, busy. Binkie's ears again, is it?'

He examined the cat carefully. 'I'm afraid she's just getting to be an old lady and isn't cleaning herself properly,' he explained. 'There's not much we can do about that. But here's more cream and I'll give her another shot of antibiotics.'

'Have you got a moment? I think I was the last in the queue.'

'Just a moment. I still have to make some visits this morning.'

'I'll be quick then. Remember Chloe Pearson? I met up with her the other day and she's invited me to her wedding. I wondered if you'd like to come with me? She said to bring a guest.'

Charlie blushed and looked uncomfortable. He cleared his throat and started to speak. Then he stopped and coughed again.

'Err . . . well . . . the thing is . . . erm . . . '

'It's OK if you're busy and you can't make it. There'll be lots of the old crowd there. I'll soon find someone to talk to.'

'Well, actually, I'm already going to Chloe's wedding. With Gemma. I got the invitation ages ago. But at least it means you'll get to meet Gemma at last. I'm sure you'll get on really well.'

'I see. Fine.'

She wished the floor would swallow her up. She wished she had never asked him and even began to wish she hadn't agreed to go to the wedding at all. She should have realised that Chloe would have invited Charlie. They had been friends along with a whole crowd of teenagers from school.

Rachel said a hurried cheerio, gathered up Binkie and the tube of cream, and headed for the door.

'Wait!' Charlie called after her. 'Wait. Let's meet up tonight and talk about it. Maybe we could all go to the wedding together and share transport?'

'Not a good idea. Sorry. And I'm busy tonight. 'Bye. See you soon.'

She rushed out of the waiting-room and the receptionist called after her, 'Rachel! Rachel, wait a minute. You haven't paid.'

'Send me a bill,' Rachel called back, wanting to be as far away from Charlie as fast as possible.

Drat Gemma!

Rachel and Charlie had been getting on so well, and now she had to face meeting Gemma, and Charlie was naïve enough to think they might actually get on! He was truly insensitive if he hadn't realised how Rachel felt. But perhaps it wasn't really his fault. She had been pretending that being friends with him was enough for her and that it didn't matter about his relationship with this woman.

'What on earth is wrong?' her mother said as she arrived back at the shop. 'Oh, no! It's Binkie, isn't it?' She grabbed the pet carrier and peered in. 'Oh! She looks all right. So what is it, love?'

'I'm being silly, Mum. I just asked Charlie if he'd like to go with me to the wedding and he's already been invited and he's taking Gemma. I guess she suddenly became a reality and I've been fooling myself into thinking she was only around in the background.'

'I'm sorry. Maybe there's someone else who'd like to go with you?'

'Who else do I know around here these days? It's all right. I'm sure there'll be lots of the old crowd there. I won't be on my own for long.'

'And you've got a lovely outfit. You'll look gorgeous. Now, are you in this evening?'

'Where would I be going? And why do you ask?'

'It's just that your dad and I want to have a chat with you.'

'This sounds ominous. Is there something wrong?'

'No, no. It's nothing to worry about. Please, let's wait till we can all sit down together and talk properly. Oh, here's someone coming in for coffee. I don't want to say anything more just now.'

Rachel went back to the cottage, her mind still whirling from the encounter at the vet's. And what on earth could her parents want to talk to her about? She hoped it wasn't something else wrong with her mother's eyes.

She let the cat out and made herself some coffee. She wanted a little time on her own to try to come to terms with her silly predicament.

Meeting Gemma

Audrey and Jack refused to discuss anything until they had all finished supper that evening.

Then, once the dishes were stacked in the sink, Jack went to make coffee, as usual.

'Come on then. What's the big mystery?' asked Rachel.

'The thing is, we've had a letter.'

Rachel stared. They had letters all the time.

'From the people who own the craft centre place up the road.'

'What do they want? To buy all our stock so they have something genuine to sell?'

'It's more than that. They want to buy our shop.'

'What? Don't tell me you're thinking about it? Oh, Mum! Dad! No! You can't be.'

'It sounds like a reasonable offer. Lock, stock and barrel. They want the lot.'

'But you'd hate living here and seeing someone else running it every day. What would you do with yourselves? You'd be bored to tears.'

'I'm not sure we would. We could sell the cottage too, and move to a nice modern bungalow.'

'Oh! So, what have they offered?'

They pushed a sheet of paper towards her and she scanned the words and figures. Then she pulled a face.

'You have to be joking. You can't accept this. The shop's worth at least half as much again.'

Audrey took the letter back.

'But listen — they say, 'In view of the increased local competition it is unlikely that the property will realise any more than our substantial offer. In fact, the value is more likely to decrease as a going concern. You would be advised to accept this offer while it stands.' See?'

'They're just trying it on. Even if it

wasn't a going concern, a property like this, in a prime position in a popular village, is worth far more than they're offering. Honestly. You can't seriously even consider it. With Auntie Marjorie's generous gifts, we're going to make a nice sum of money. There's heaps we can do to improve the shop. If you want to have more time to yourselves then I'm happy to take on more responsibility and even run the business for you if you'd let me. With a bit of help from time to time, I'm sure I could manage it myself. Anyway, I can hardly imagine we're a threat to them. I mean to say, we're just a small shop and they have something bordering on a restaurant rather than a cream tea outlet.'

'I suppose we did really hope for a bit more. I doubt we could live on the proceeds of this offer, however carefully it was invested. And if you really do want to stay here and work with us, then I don't see we have a choice, do you, Audrey?'

'No. Of course not. As you say, we'd

probably be very bored after a little while. It's agreed then. We write back and tell Cornwall Developments, who-ever they are, to get lost.'

Though Audrey spoke emphatically, Rachel sensed disappointment in her mother's voice. Perhaps she really did want to give up the shop and retire. But that was a wild thought. She couldn't imagine her parents without Cranhams' Curios.

'I suppose we'd better wash up and see what's on TV tonight.'

'I'm going to do a bit of work on the website and then I'll sort out our latest auctions,' said Rachel. 'There are a couple of sales finishing tonight and we'll be collecting Marjorie's stuff soon so I need to prepare for the influx of fresh stock.'

She went up to her room and worked offline for a while, then she needed to connect to the phone socket so she took her laptop downstairs to the dining-room. From there she could hear her parents talking. She couldn't hear what they were saying, but their voices sounded slightly agitated. But she knew she was right. The offer from Cornwall Developments was paltry in the extreme, and if her mum and dad really wanted to sell up, they must wait for a much better offer.

She completed her tasks and went to join her parents, who immediately stopped talking and settled to watch the TV. There was a slightly uneasy silence for the rest of the evening.

'If you want me to write the letter to the craft centre people on the computer, just let me know. It will look more professional if I print it out with a proper letter heading and everything. Just tell me what you want me to say.'

'Thanks, love. We'll look at it in the morning. But with all your experience, I'm sure you can manage it yourself.'

'OK. I'll run off a first draft tomorrow and let you see it. I'm off to bed now. Sleep well. Night, night.'

★ ★ ★

But Rachel couldn't sleep. Her mind was still whirling with thoughts of Chloe's wedding, takeover bids, and her disastrous romantic dreams of a life with Charlie.

She gave up lying awake and got up to write the letter to Cornwall Developments.

Once that was done, she managed to fall asleep, and only woke when the smell of coffee permeated her brain. She printed off the letter and took it downstairs with her.

'My word, that looks most professional. Thank you, dear. There's just one thing though — you've said that we would never entertain the idea of such an offer. Actually, we might consider it if it was for a lot more money.'

'That's no problem. I can alter it to say whatever you like. It's easy to change one line. I kept the first draft on the computer and it only takes seconds to do it.'

'More of your clever technology! More things I don't understand. When your father types a letter it's a mess of white paint stuff and the air is blue with his mutterings. Then he usually starts again from scratch.'

Once the letter of refusal had been posted, Rachel busied herself with thinking how best to display the new stock that Marjorie had gifted to them. They were due to collect the items in a few days time and she'd given a lot of thought to how best to prepare the shelves for their display, so she decided to pop out to buy the bits and pieces of trimmings that she needed to carry out her ideas.

As she left the shop, Charlie drove by and stopped a little way past her. She tried to pretend she hadn't seen him but he shouted her name.

'Hello, stranger. I haven't seen you properly for a while. I wondered if you fancy a trip to the beach this afternoon? I'm taking a bit of time off and thought that as it's such a nice day, I might pick up a picnic lunch. What do you say?'

'It sounds nice, but I'm really busy

just now. Thanks anyway.'

'Please. I'll get some stuff from the deli. Please, Rachel. Don't cut me off.'

Against her better judgement, she found herself agreeing to join him.

'I'll collect you around one o'clock. See you later.'

He drove away and she cursed herself for being so weak willed.

She went into the newsagents and bought some coloured paper to line the shelves and saw a box of fairy-lights reduced to half price. On impulse, she bought them too, planning to put them round the window to cheer the place up in the evenings. If people were walking around the village when it was getting dark and saw a bit of light and colour, then it might tempt them to come back the next day for a closer look.

She was determined that the generous gifts from her mother's friend should be something of a turning point. With all the free stock they had to sell, and the Internet auctions, she must surely increase the shop's profits.

And there was always the local auction room. They'd sold her parents' pieces of furniture very successfully. The chairs had realised over a thousand pounds and the bureau had gone for over five hundred, so they had been very pleased with the results.

She decided to suggest taking her mother to the auction room again soon. They hadn't been for ages, and they used to have such fun at one time, buying boxes of junk for next to nothing and then seeing what was in them. They'd been lucky on several occasions, finding plates and items of jewellery that had sold well in the shop. Larger items of furniture and such like wouldn't fit into their restricted space, but jewellery was always popular.

As soon as she got back to the shop she mentioned her ideas to her parents, who looked a bit doubtful but weren't about to argue.

'Oh, and I'm having lunch with Charlie. We're having a picnic!'

'But, I thought . . . ' Audrey began.

Then she gave a shrug. She had more to worry about than the on-off situation with her daughter and the vet.

'I hope it doesn't rain. It looks a bit threatening.'

Rachel set about fixing up the lights round the window, watched carefully by her father.

'It isn't Christmas, is it? Have I got my seasons all wrong?'

'I thought it might be nice to have some lights in the window in the evenings. This place looks dead once it's closed. I know it might seem a bit tacky but it was a cheap option. Once we've started making a good profit again, we should go for some spotlights and maybe a new sign outside.'

'Well, if you think it might help. I'm not happy to spend much money though, not until we know how things are going to go once the craft centre is really up and running during the season.'

★ ★ ★

The rain began as they were driving down the beach lane, so they sat in Charlie's Range Rover to eat the picnic. He'd really splashed out and bought locally smoked salmon, home-made paté and fresh rolls.

'Wow. This is a real feast!. Thank you for taking such trouble.'

'I haven't, not really. The village deli has an excellent range of goodies so it was just a case of buying what seemed appropriate. Cheers.'

'Cheers. Charlie . . . I'm sorry about the other day. Of course I should have realised you'd be going to Chloe's wedding and that you'd be taking Gemma. It'll be nice to meet her.'

She nearly choked on the words but she knew she needed to be grown up about the whole thing.

'Good. I'm glad you feel that way. So, why don't we all travel together?'

'I don't think that would be a good idea. We might not want to leave at the same time.'

'As you like. I was thinking more

about being able to have a drink and not worry about driving.'

'A good thought but I might get my dad to fetch and carry me. I'm sure he would. Or I'll splash out on a taxi just for once.'

'So, who will you take as your guest?'

'Oh, I'll not bother. I'll just rely on knowing people when I get there.' She laughed. 'I can't imagine scatty Chloe as a married woman, can you?'

'She's calmed down a lot. Mike's a really nice guy. Their place is going to be lovely, too. It's a barn conversion in the gardens of her brother's house, Sea Haven. You know it?'

'I remember it being a tumbledown old place once. Chloe babbled on about it all when I met her. This paté is gorgeous.'

They chatted more easily as Charlie brought out some early strawberries and chocolate éclairs for pudding, and Rachel was in heaven.

'My very favourites.'

'I remembered.'

'Oh, Charlie, you are thoughtful.'

Impulsively she leaned over and kissed his cheek.

He hesitated, and then put his arms round her and kissed her on the lips.

'Oh, Charlie!'

'I'm sorry. I shouldn't have done that,' he said, drawing back. 'Sorry.'

'I'm not,' she murmured. 'Sorry, I mean.'

'I'm not being fair to you. Come on, eat up.'

The moment was gone.

She finished her éclair, hardly tasting it. Then, because the rain had stopped, they went for a walk along the beach.

The sea was rolling in, with huge breakers crashing against the rocks and sending up spray several feet into the air. Suddenly feeling reckless, Rachel ran along the sand and allowed herself to get covered in spray. She laughed delightedly at the freedom she was feeling. She knew for certain now that she could never go back to her old life in London, even if her new life had to be lived without Charlie.

'You're a mad woman. Soaking wet and quite crazy. Will you never grow up?'

'Oh, I'm grown up already, Charlie. I think I'm just happy to be in my natural surroundings. This is where I was always meant to be. It took all those years away for me to know it, and now I want to shout it aloud.'

She looked back at him. He had a strange expression on his face, wistful but happy.

He grinned and caught her hand, dragging her back into the spray which soaked them both.

'Now who's mad? You're a respectable village vet and you're behaving like the teenager I used to know.'

He paused and looked at her again, almost as if he was seeing her for the first time. He kissed her wet cheek and dragged her away from the water.

'I think we'd better go home and get into some dry clothes. Or we'll both get pneumonia and neither of us will be attending this wedding on Saturday.'

★ ★ ★

By the time Saturday arrived, Rachel was feeling far less confident. She got herself ready rather too early and wandered round the shop, picking things up and putting them down, and driving her mother to distraction.

'Do you want your father to run you over there now?' Audrey suggested.

'Not really, I'd only be hanging around at the hotel. I bet Chloe's place is a hive of activity. Everyone dashing round madly and yelling at each other. Make-up and hairspray everywhere. The kids will be excited. I think her niece, Sarah, is a bridesmaid and her nephew, Carl, is being an usher. He's only a kid but he refused to be a page boy. Not cool enough for a teenager.'

'I'm sure you'll have a lovely time. Did you say Charlie's going? Why didn't you go together?'

194

'He's taking Gemma.'

The penny dropped for Audrey. This was the reason for her daughter's nerves and probably why she'd been like a bear with a sore head since the picnic. Pity. He'd make the perfect match for her.

'I'm sure you'll enjoy yourself, though,' she said reassuringly. 'You and Chloe are such old friends, and I expect you'll know most people there. Now, do you want a coffee before you leave?'

'No, thanks, Mum. Maybe I will see if Dad's ready and then we can go. There's bound to be someone around for me to talk to.'

★ ★ ★

The hotel where the wedding was taking place overlooked the sea. It was a civil ceremony and they had a licenced wedding room, dedicated for the purpose. Rachel found a whole group of old friends standing around in the foyer. There were squeals of 'Hello!'

and 'Haven't seen you in ages!' and 'Heard you were back!'

Gradually, everyone drifted towards the wedding room and found seats.

Rachel found herself sitting next to two old school friends and, as they chatted, she watched the door carefully. But it wasn't the arrival of the bride she was looking out for. She was anxious to catch a first glimpse Gemma, if only to prepare herself for facing her in person.

'So, what do you think?' one of her friends was asking.

'Sorry? Oh! There's Charlie Williams coming in.'

'Wow! Who's that woman with him?'

Rachel stared. Gemma was gorgeous. She could quite see why Charlie was smitten. A striking redhead, she was wearing a pale lilac silk dress and a matching hat that perched on top of her mass of curls.

Everything about her breathed style, and Rachel felt positively dowdy in her simple skirt and jacket. She had chosen not to wear a hat but had left her hair hanging loose with a flower tucked in at one side. She felt underdressed and very provincial in comparison to her rival.

Charlie spotted her and gave her a wave as he ushered Gemma to a seat near the back.

The loudspeaker system switched from playing a gentle, classical piece to the Wedding March, and Rachel suddenly realised that she hadn't even noticed the groom and best man at the front of the room.

Mike *did* look nice, but nervous — a tall good-looking man in a formal suit.

Then Chloe came into the room looking wonderful in a slim-fitting creamy white creation with a long, flowing veil held in place with a wreath of wild flowers. Perfect for Chloe, Rachel thought.

The couple made their vows and the simple ceremony brought tears to the eyes of most of their friends. Poems were read out that had been specially written for the occasion. Then the bride and groom turned and walked from the room, looking so happy that they triggered another bout of tearfulness from their guests.

Everyone began to move out into the lobby where drinks were being offered.

'You look wonderful, Chloe,' Rachel told her friend when she managed to snatch a word with the bride and groom. 'Makes such a change from jeans and tatty T-shirts.'

They both laughed.

'Lovely to meet you, Mike!'

Then, unable to avoid the moment any longer, Rachel crossed the room to speak to Charlie and Gemma.

Charlie made the introductions, looking at her anxiously.

'Hello, Gemma,' she said politely, holding out her hand.

'And hello to you, Rachel,' Gemma said coolly, with a formal touch of fingers. Rachel felt as if the woman was afraid of catching something if she really held her hand. 'Charlie told me how you used to play together as kids.'

Rachel winced slightly at the words but decided against registering her protest. She glanced at Charlie who lowered his eyes, looking most uncomfortable — and gorgeous, Rachel thought — in his dark suit and grey silk tie. Even his hair looked neatly tamed for once.

'Lovely room, isn't it?' She found herself chattering on. 'Magnificent view. That's one of the greatest surfing beaches in Cornwall out there. In the whole country, probably.'

'Not quite my thing, surfing,' Gemma said in a stiff voice.

'No. You're more into digging holes in the ground, aren't you?'

Rachel lowered her eyes as she spoke the words, hating herself for being as bitchy as Gemma sounded.

'Are you going to get me a drink, darling?' Gemma asked Charlie as she turned away, openly snubbing Rachel, and moved on to another group of people, presumably more to her liking.

Well, thought Rachel, Gemma may

look sensational but she didn't deserve someone as lovely as Charlie. She joined a group of her own friends.

'That went well,' Amy, one of her group remarked.

'You noticed,' Rachel replied grimly.

'I'd heard you were seeing each other again. You and Charlie. So who's that woman, then?'

'Someone he met at university. I gather they're almost engaged.'

'Hardly the vet's wife type. What does she do?'

'Lectures in archaeology.'

'I always thought you and Charlie would get married yourselves. Still, after your years in London, I suppose you're used to the high life. Boring old St Truan would never satisfy you.'

'Actually, it does. And yes, I suppose I did have some sort of hopes that Charlie and I could get together again. But as he says, we're just good mates these days.'

'Ladies and gentlemen, please take your seats. The seating plan is inside the door. Enjoy your meal.' The manager was dressed in a formal black coat and was taking charge personally.

They all trooped into the large dining-room and looked for their places.

To Rachel's horror, Charlie was placed between herself and Gemma. Not very tactful of Chloe but she clearly hadn't realised the situation. The rest of the old school group were also at the table so at least there were plenty of other people to talk to.

By the time they reached the main course, the only person looking really uncomfortable was Gemma herself. She did relax a little but clearly felt out of place. Charlie did his best to look after her and also to give some attention to the others, especially Rachel.

At last the meal was over, coffee was served, and the speeches began.

Finally, champagne and wedding cake were brought round and people were free to get up from their tables and drift around the room to speak to the other guests.

Once the dancing started, Rachel was never off her feet. She began to enjoy herself. She kept an eye on Charlie and Gemma, and although the two of them did make their way on to the dance floor once or twice, dancing was clearly an activity that Gemma disliked.

At long last, Charlie made his way over to Rachel to ask for a dance, and they melted together as perfectly as they had done as teenagers. He spun her round the room as the music finished and she collapsed against him, laughing.

'Thank you. That was fun.'

'We still dance well together, don't we?' he said.

'We learned together. Miss Francis did a good job,' she said, laughing, remembering the highly embarrassing dance lessons at school.

'Another?' he asked.

'Not a good idea. Your partner looks far from happy. She's looking daggers at me. You didn't tell me what a stunner she is! Gorgeous outfit.'

'Maybe a bit too formal though, for Cornwall.'

'Weddings *are* formal. A chance to dress up.'

'Well, you look lovely, Rachel. That outfit really suits you.'

'Thank you. But you really ought to get back to your girlfriend.'

'I . . . well, maybe you're right. See you soon?'

'Maybe.'

★ ★ ★

By eleven o'clock, Rachel felt exhausted and phoned her father to ask him to collect her. Charlie and Gemma had left already.

She said goodbye to everyone and stood waiting in the foyer.

Her emotions were jangled and she was almost tearful.

Gemma was real. Gemma was beautiful, stylish, and obviously very bright, if a little bitchy.

Rachel had subconsciously been hoping that her rival would be dowdy, dressed in a baggy sweater, and have wire-rimmed glasses perched on the end of her nose — not the woman who had clung so tightly to Charlie's arm.

It was time for Rachel to move on, emotionally, if not physically.

Something To Celebrate

On that Sunday morning, the Cranhams had a phone call from Marjorie. She was moving out of her house on the following Tuesday and had finally sorted out which of her particular treasures to take with her. She would like them to come and collect the rest of her things as soon as possible.

'Well, if you're really sure,' Audrey told her, 'the three of us could come round after lunch today.'

'That would be wonderful. Could you bring some boxes? I've got plenty of newspaper for wrapping but all my boxes have been used up. I never knew I had so much rubbish in my life.'

It took Audrey, Jack and Rachel the best part of the afternoon to pack up everything. There were three china tea-services besides endless other pieces of porcelain and silver.

Marjorie would listen to none of their protests about the value of everything and refused to contemplate any payment at all.

'No, my dears. It would be like selling pieces of my life if I took any money from you. This way is so much easier and nicer for me and I've more than enough money to live on.'

'I think I'd better take some of this stuff back to the shop and come back for the rest later,' Jack decided, and set off with the first van load.

When he came back with some of the boxes that he'd emptied out, they began again.

It was almost six o'clock by the time they'd finished.

'I'm shattered,' Audrey announced when they finally got back to the shop. 'I can't face sorting any of this lot out now. We'll have a blitz on it all tomorrow. Let's just make some tea and put our feet up for the rest of the evening.'

The answering machine was flashing

as they went in through the door to the cottage, and when Rachel pressed the play button, Charlie's voice filled the room.

'Rachel? I need to see you as soon as possible. Are you free this evening? Please call me back as soon as you get this message.'

'I wonder what's wrong?' she muttered. 'Why didn't he call my mobile?'

'Perhaps because you left it here,' her mother replied.

When Rachel checked, there was a message on her mobile as well.

She dialled Charlie's number.

'Charlie? Is something wrong?'

'I'm not sure it's wrong exactly. Can we talk? I could pick you up and we could go for a drink.'

'I'm pretty tired, actually. Won't it wait?'

'Not really.'

'Well, all right. Just a quick drink.' She put her hand over the phone. 'You don't mind, do you, Mum?'

'Of course not, love.'

'OK, Charlie. See you in an hour.' She put down the phone. 'I must have a shower. I'm all hot and sweaty.'

* * *

She stood under the running water and wondered what Charlie had to say to her that was so important it couldn't wait until the next day.

Most likely that he and Gemma had finally got engaged. Weddings often sparked a spate of proposals.

They went to a quiet pub in the next village. Charlie even switched off his mobile and he chose a corner table where nobody could overhear them. He ordered toasted sandwiches for them both as Rachel said she didn't want much to eat.

'What's so urgent?' she asked.

'I wanted to ask you where you thought our relationship was going and how you felt about the future?'

'I see. Nothing much to discuss there, then.'

'Don't be flippant. Gemma and I, well, we had a long talk after the wedding. It seems there are some major difficulties for us. Though we've been together for several years, neither of us seems able to make a commitment. I want to be here and she wants to be in Bristol. Our work, you see.'

'Surely if you love each other, the work situation can be resolved?'

'That's just it. I don't think we've ever really loved each other. If we did then surely we'd want to be together more than we are? It's like neighbours who get on really well when they're neighbours, but if either of them move on, they discover the only thing they had in common was living near each other.'

'So, what did the two of you decide to do?' she asked, wondering if she dared hope that their decision was the right one for her.

'We've decided not to contact each other for a few weeks and then see how we feel about the situation. See whether we've missed each other.'

'OK. So where does this leave me? Us?'

He was prevented from answering as the food arrived.

Rachel looked at the sandwiches and knew she'd never manage to swallow so much as a single bite.

'Where do you want it to leave us?' Charlie asked, after the waitress had walked away.

'I think you must have some idea of how I feel about you. But I don't want to make a fool of myself if you don't feel the same.'

Why, oh, why hadn't he and Gemma simply made a clean break of it?

Rachel felt as if she wasn't much better off than she had been before. A sort of second best. But would she rather be second best than nothing at all?

'I'm very fond of you, Rachel,' he went on. 'In fact, I suspect if it wasn't for you, Gemma and I would go on like we have been for ever, without ever making a proper commitment. You've made the difference. In fact, seeing you both together at Chloe's wedding, I'm not sure I even wanted her there. I'd so much rather have gone there with you. So what do you think?'

Her mind was racing. It was on the tip of her tongue to say that she would only continue to see Charlie if the Gemma situation was resolved, but she knew she couldn't bear to go without seeing him, even if it meant she would still be in the other girl's shadow.

'I think it would be great to spend some time together, but I don't think we should hurry things. After all, you haven't really finished with Gemma, have you? Now, I think you should eat the rest of that food or it will be cold and revolting.'

'You're being wonderful about all this, Rachel. Really, I mean it. I do so enjoy spending time with you and I want it to go on.'

'Fine. Now eat.'

★ ★ ★

Over the next few weeks, Rachel spent most of her time either revamping the displays in the shop by setting out Marjorie's treasures to their best advantage, or selling lots of things on the auction sites.

They were making a good profit at last and she suggested some improvements to the shop. But her parents still said they didn't want to do anything drastic until they had spent a whole season with the competition down the road.

Marjorie was settling down really well in her new apartment and loved the fact that she had little or no housework to do, and could see people whenever she liked.

'You'd hate not having enough to do, though, wouldn't you, Mum?'

'Maybe,' Audrey said rather wistfully. 'But I do get a little sick of making scones every day.'

'Don't make any then. Or put some in the freezer for the next day.'

'Not allowed. They wouldn't be fresh

then, would they? Are you in or out this evening?'

'Out. Charlie and I are going to that new place on the Truro road. It's supposed to be really good.'

'It must be costing Charlie a fortune, taking you out to eat out all the time.'

★　★　★

They arrived at the new pub restaurant and ordered a pasta dish each.

Rachel brought Charlie up to speed on how she'd been getting on in the shop.

'So, the craft centre hasn't caused as much of a problem as you thought?'

'Well, not so far, but we've been given so much free stock lately that it's difficult to tell whether our profits would normally have been down. I don't think the shop's been as busy as it would have been before the craft centre opened. But it's so long since I spent a whole summer at home that it's difficult to judge. I just wish I knew who was behind Cornwall Developments and why they made us such a ludicrous offer for the shop.'

Charlie looked uncomfortable.

'Antiques apart, how are you feeling now?'

'What do you mean exactly?'

'Well, we've been seeing a lot of each other lately and, so far, we seem to have kept each other at arm's length.'

'I thought that's how you wanted it.'

'I'm beginning to think I want more from our relationship. I've hardly thought of Gemma in days. Weeks even. I'm wondering if I ought to go to see her and finally tidy things up.'

'What a way of putting it — 'tidy things up'! Do you mean end your relationship with her?'

Her voice shook slightly as she spoke and her heart raced madly within her chest, making breathing difficult.

'To put it bluntly, yes. I know now that I don't love her. Never really came close to it.'

'I see,' she almost squeaked.

Did that mean he loved her?

'What do you think?'

'It's rather up to you, isn't it?'

'But do you feel the same about me as I feel about you?'

'I'm not sure.'

He looked crestfallen at her words.

Rachel cleared her throat and looked him in the eye.

'I'm not sure how you feel about me. You've never told me. So I can't say if I feel the same as you or not.'

Her cheeks were burning a fiery red. She was saved further embarrassment by the arrival of the food.

'I'm not doing very well, am I?' Charlie said as they began to eat. 'I'm no good at emotions. I think what I'm trying to say is that I love you, Rachel.'

'Did you want sauce with that?' The waitress, unnoticed by either of them, had returned to their table with a tray of condiments.

'No, thanks,' Charlie spluttered.

Rachel began to laugh until tears were rolling down her cheeks as the pent-up tension was broken.

'I've never been asked anything so unromantic at such an inappropriate moment,' she finally managed to say.

'So, what do you feel about me?' he persisted.

'Of course I love you. Always have done.'

He reached across the table and took her hand. He pressed it to his lips and she felt her heart soar. This was what she had been dreaming of. She found her voice had deserted her and so she just smiled and squeezed his hand.

'Don't let this hurry things. I'd still like plenty of time to get to know you all over again. I'm just delighted that we've cleared the air and I know where I stand with you. Now, all I have to do is try to sort out the parents and their business.'

'Ever practical. I tell you I love you and you're still worrying about your mum and dad's shop.'

'Sorry. But face it, you'd have been a bit disturbed if I'd gone all super romantic and over the top. So what happens now? I mean, when are you seeing Gemma to break things off with her?'

'I thought I might drive up to Bristol on Saturday morning. Then we can talk it through and I'll drive right back in the evening.'

She felt nervous about this arrangement, though she knew it had to be done.

* * *

Saturday was a tense day and she'd heard nothing from Charlie by the time she went to bed. Maybe he'd changed his mind when he'd seen Gemma again or maybe she'd made a fuss.

It was a long night.

'Are you all right, love?' her father asked next morning. 'You look shattered. Didn't you sleep?'

'Not really.'

Both parents looked concerned and her mother poured her more coffee.

'Actually, Mum — Dad, we need to talk. Charlie's driven up to Bristol and is finally finishing with Gemma. And he says he loves me.'

'Why, that's wonderful, darling! We're both fond of Charlie and it means you'll stay on in the area. If you get married, I mean.'

'Hey, hang on. You're jumping the gun a bit. We'll have no talk of weddings yet, please. I've no idea if it will work out. But as for staying in the area, well, yes, I do want to do that. I'd like to make Cranhams' Curios a real success. I'm sure I can do it and I'm sure the business could make enough to keep us all.

'I admit that I'm probably being a nuisance to you by living here . . . no, you don't have to protest, Mum. As soon as it's practical, I'd like to find a place of my own. You don't want me hanging around indefinitely.'

'You'll be lucky to find anywhere to live down here. Prices have gone through the roof. Cornwall property prices compare to parts of London these days.'

'Well, I can look around. If we go on doing as well as we have lately, there should be a bit more money to spare. You'll probably be able to pay me a salary soon.'

'But . . . well, perhaps you're right.' Audrey felt helpless. She couldn't say what was in her mind and allow Rachel to think she wasn't wanted. 'And perhaps your dad and I could start taking things more easily. We could have the occasional day off, couldn't we, Jack?'

'Maybe we could. We could even leave Rachel in charge and have a bit of a holiday?'

'That would be great!' Rachel was delighted. 'Just what I hoped you might do. Meanwhile, no fancy ideas about Charlie and me. I know I do love him but then, I think I always have. But I'm not sure about the marriage word. I'm just not ready.'

'Whatever you say.'

Audrey exchanged glances with her husband and gave him a grin. Whatever Rachel said about marriage, she knew her daughter would settle down before too long passed. What was to stop her? She'd got the London career thing out of her system, and had admitted she had moved back permanently. Cornwall did that to people. How many folks did she know who had come for holidays and then moved here permanently?

* * *

It seemed an eternity before the phone rang and Charlie was on the other end of the line, letting Rachel know that he'd returned home safely from Bristol.

He and Gemma had had a long talk and Gemma had admitted to feeling relieved that their relationship was over. She would never have been part of his life in Cornwall because she didn't want to move away from her own life and work in Bristol. But Charlie could never have found as good a position in

Bristol as the one he had working with his father — not at his age.

'We had a meal together, for old times' sake, so I was late back. What did you want to do today?'

'You mean you're off for two whole days? No sick animals to care for?'

'Well, I might have to offer to be on call. Dad coped yesterday but there were no real emergencies.'

'We could go for a walk or something.'

'Good idea! It's looking like a lovely day. How about we climb to the top of the St Truan Beacon? I'd like to take some pictures from up there. I Haven't been up there in ages.'

'OK.'

'Is that Charlie, dear?' her mother asked, coming in from the kitchen.

Rachel covered the mouthpiece.

'Yes. We're going for a walk.'

'Lovely. Why don't you bring him back for lunch? There's plenty and it would be nice to see him again.'

Rachel frowned. She didn't want him

to feel pressured by family visits, not at this early stage.

'Rachel?' Charlie almost shouted down the phone. 'I heard your mother's invitation and yes, please. That would be great.'

'He heard and said yes, please.' She grinned at her mother. 'See you soon,' she said as she put the phone down.

★   ★   ★

Rachel's mind was a churning mass of feelings as she went in search of a lightweight anorak.

The huge sense of relief she had been expecting to feel once Charlie and Gemma were no longer an item simply hadn't come.

She sensed there was still something not quite right.

Just lately, at times, Charlie could be quite secretive and it seemed to her as if he was holding something back. But perhaps her imagination was just too active.

With a small sigh, she put on her old walking boots and headed off down the drive to wait for Charlie to arrive and, when she saw his Range Rover coming up the High Street, she couldn't help feeling a lurch of bubbling excitement.

'This isn't what I call walking,' she protested as she climbed into the passenger seat.

'I thought I'd better bring a change of clothes, and anyhow, if we walk all the way to Beacon and then climb it, we might not be back in time for lunch.'

'Always thinking of your stomach. But it's a good idea.'

They parked in the nearest lay-by to the track that led up to the top of what was the highest hill in the area. Not exactly a mountain, but the Beacon was a rugged climb with spectacular views from the top, over the sea and the surrounding land.

They were both breathless as they climbed and Charlie reached for her hand. It felt good. She was suddenly filled with the feeling that everything was going to work out and she laughed out loud with the exhilaration of the morning and everything that was happening.

She let out a loud whoop.

'It is a bit like that today, isn't it?' Charlie shouted and let out a whoop of his own.

They both laughed at their own silliness, and ran up the final bit of path to the summit.

There was a stone marker at the top and Rachel clambered on to it.

'Good morning, Cornwall!' she yelled, and waved her arms in the air. 'Just in case anyone has binoculars trained on me,' she told Charlie.

They both laughed, their happiness filling them both. Then they fell silent and absorbed the beauty that stretched before them.

'Look, there are some little sailing dinghies right out at sea.'

'And a tanker over there on the horizon. Massive thing. Probably bigger than some of our villages, I'm sure.'

'You can even see the clay hills at St Austell from here. Amazing. They're miles away.'

'I'm so glad you came back, Rachel. It was meant to be. Come here.'

He pulled her into his arms and tenderly, gently, kissed her lips. It felt almost as though they were flying together as the wind whipped around them.

They stood on the top of their world, wrapped in each other's arms, and watched the glorious scenery for several minutes.

'Oh, drat,' he said suddenly. 'I forgot to bring my camera to take those pictures I wanted. I'm designing new headed paper for the practice and wanted a picture taken from the top of the Beacon to use for our logo.'

'Then we'll just have to climb back up here soon, won't we?'

Slowly they walked down again, hand in hand.

★ ★ ★

Jack and Audrey had made a great effort with lunch. Their best china and cutlery were laid out in the dining-room and the meal was cooked to perfection.

'I hope they're not late. The beef is just right and the Yorkshire puddings are nice and crisp. I don't want them going soggy. Can you see Charlie's car yet, Jack?'

'Yes. His Range Rover's just squeezing into the drive. Not much room for it. It's a big vehicle.'

'I'll put the veg on. Have you got a drink ready to offer?'

'Yes, dear, but please stop fussing and relax.'

'I don't want him thinking I can't do things properly.'

'Oh, for goodness' sake. How many meals have you given Charlie in the old days?'

'Well, it's different now. He's all grown up and he's the vet. Why aren't they coming in?'

'Oh, dear! They seem to be arguing

about something. No, it's all right. They're getting out of the car now.'

'Charlie wanted to change but I said he was fine as he is,' Rachel announced as they burst in through the back door.

'And thank you for inviting me, Mrs Cranham. Much appreciated. There's nothing like a roast on a Sunday.'

'Oh, doesn't your mother cook then?'

'I don't actually live with my parents. I have a flat at their house, over the surgery.'

'I didn't know that,' Audrey said in surprise. 'I just assumed you lived with them.'

'No. We decided that my coming back here would never work out unless I had my own space. We had the store room and attic converted so I'm completely independent. It isn't huge but it's quite adequate.'

'I see. Now, who's for a sherry or a glass of wine?'

'Not for me, thanks. I'm driving, so I'll just have water for now and maybe a small glass of wine with the meal?'

It was a pleasant, light-hearted meal, though Rachel was a little concerned that her parents were making too much of the occasion. They seemed to be making assumptions about her relationship with Charlie and it was still very early days.

'Tell me, Charlie, have you visited that new craft place yet?' Audrey asked cheerfully.

His face fell and he looked very uncomfortable.

'Well, yes.'

'And what do you think of it?'

'Quite smart. They seem to be doing a lot of trade. The car park's usually full.'

His voice tailed off as he saw their expressions. Clearly it was not what they wanted to hear.

'But it's nothing like your shop. Most of their stuff is reproduction, not the genuine article like the antiques that you sell.' He paused. 'That was a wonderful meal, Mrs Cranham. Thank you very much.'

'Call me Audrey,' she said. 'Can't be doing with all this formality. Help me clear, Jack, will you?'

'Why do you always look so shifty whenever the new craft centre's mentioned?' asked Rachel after her parents had disappeared into the kitchen. 'I think you're hiding something.'

'Not now, Rachel, please. Excuse me,' he apologised as his mobile phone rang. 'Dad? Yes, I will. Will it wait? OK. Give me half an hour.'

He switched the phone off.

'I'm sorry, but I have to go. Someone's bringing in a dog with a severe breathing problem. It's a young-ish puppy and Dad's concerned it might need an operation and he'll need me to help. I do apologise.'

'Oh, are you leaving?' Audrey asked as she came back into the room with a tray of coffee.

'Yes, I'm sorry. There's an emergency at the surgery that Dad can't manage alone. I hope you'll forgive me.'

'Of course. At least you managed your meal without being disturbed.'

They saw him off and sat down to drink the cooling coffee.

Helping Charlie

It was early evening when Charlie phoned to say that the operation he and his father had performed that afternoon had been a success. He sounded exhausted and made no suggestions to Rachel about meeting again that day.

'How was the little dog?' she asked.

'He's fine now, but it was awful at the time. It was such a delicate operation. I couldn't find the reason for his rasping and did an ultra-sound. He'd managed to swallow a long piece of grass and it had got stuck. He was so tiny, one slip of the scalpel and I could have finished him off. Anyway, it all went well and he's recovering.'

'Well done.'

'Now I must get to bed. I'm shattered. After the late night yesterday, all the driving to Bristol and back, and then our long walk — I've had it.

Thank your parents again for the lovely lunch and I'll see you soon. 'Night, love.'

''Night, Charlie.'

*   *   *

The next few days seemed slightly unreal to Rachel. She had to keep pinching herself from time to time to make sure that she wasn't dreaming. It was so good to know that she and Charlie at last had a relationship that she could rely on.

Her parents were enthusiastic about him, and his parents had invited her to a meal at their home on the following Saturday evening. She wasn't sure how much she should be looking forward to it as he had warned her that his mother wasn't much of a cook, and she'd always felt slightly intimidated by his father, who was rather a large man with a booming voice.

It was early Tuesday morning when her mobile rang.

'Rachel, it's Charlie. Are you busy today?'

'Not particularly. Why?'

'I wondered if you could do me the biggest favour. Claire, our receptionist, has phoned in sick — she's gone down with this fluey bug that's going around — and Mum and Dad have gone off to London for a couple of days. I'm desperate for some help here. I know it's an awful cheek, but would you be able to help out and be my receptionist? I don't want to have to close the surgery but I can't manage to answer the phones and treat the animals at the same time.'

'I think that's OK. I know Dad's got to pop out to the bank, but heck, they always managed before I came back, so I'm sure they will now. I'll just grab some breakfast and be with you as soon as I can. What time do you start?'

'Fifteen minutes ago. Tell you what, skip breakfast and I'll feed you when we have a break.'

She ran down the stairs and called

out her plans to her parents as she dashed towards the front door.

'What about toast, Rachel? Coffee?'

They stood watching, somewhat bewildered as she rushed past them.

'No time. It's a crisis over there. I'll get something later. 'Bye.'

'Why am I not surprised? She never changes. But it's good to see her so happy, isn't it?'

'I just hope it lasts. You simply never know, do you?'

*   *   *

There were several people already queueing as she went into the waiting-room. Some of them were obviously disgruntled at having being left unattended for a while.

She assumed Charlie was in the consulting room and she went behind the desk straight away. She knew roughly how the system worked, from her own visits to the surgery with Binkie, and she took the name of each person waiting, writing the names on a pad. Once they were all seated, she began to look for their record cards.

She had seen Claire do this several times and she even managed to put the coloured strips of paper into the places where the files came from so they could be easily returned after use.

Pleased with herself, she stacked the record cards, waiting for Charlie to come out and collect them.

The phone rang. She almost said 'Cranhams' Curios' when she answered it but stopped herself in time.

It was a customer wanting a home visit.

'I'm sorry, but I don't have Mr Williams' diary to hand. May I call you back a little later? If you could give me your number? Oh, Mrs Eccles. Good morning. Is it about Brutus? Are you able to tell me what the trouble seems to be? Oh, I am sorry. I'll call you back in a little while, or I'll see if Mr Williams can speak to you. Thank you. Goodbye.'

'Very impressive,' Charlie said as he came around to her side of the desk. 'I knew you could do it. Who was that?'

'Mrs Eccles. It's her old German Shepherd. He's collapsed again and she wants you to go round.'

'I'll get there as soon as surgery is over. I'm afraid she's going to have to face the big decision. I doubt there's anything more I can do for him.' He was speaking in an undertone so that the other patients couldn't hear. 'Call her back, please, and say I'll get there as soon as I can.'

'OK, I'll do it right now.' She handed him a record card. 'I think it's this one next. What do I do about people paying?'

'I'll give each patient a slip with the charges noted on it. Some people have accounts and if that's the case, then you need to write the amount into the book there. Don't worry if you haven't time. You can always leave the slips in an envelope and I can fill in the book later. Thanks again for helping out.'

She was kept busy for the next hour. People and pets came and went and she seemed to be keeping track of everything. The phone rang every few minutes and she ended up with a list of numbers to call back.

Mrs Eccles had been upset but grateful that Charlie could go round so soon, but Rachel know that the poor lady was going to be devastated at the loss of her pet.

Looking at some of the cards pinned to the noticeboard, she spotted an appeal for someone to give a home to a five-year-old mongrel. The current owner sounded desperate. She was moving house and there was no room for the dog at her new place. Tomorrow was the deadline for re-homing the dog, and it would have to be put down if a home couldn't be found.

The notice began: *URGENT. Loving mongrel bitch needs a new home. Well trained, well behaved and the perfect companion.'*

Poor dog and poor lady. Rachel was

almost inclined to give it a home herself, except that she didn't have a place of her own, and Binkie — not to mention her parents — would be furious.

How could Charlie cope with such emotional wrenches all the time?

But Rachel had an idea. Perhaps Mrs Eccles could be persuaded to take the dog. She was going to be devastated when her old friend had to be put down, and answering this plea for help from another distraught dog lover could be the answer. Wisely, she kept her idea to herself until she had time to discuss it with Charlie.

'Shall I come with you to see Brutus?' she offered.

'I really need you to stay here and field the phone calls — at least until midday. I'm usually here till then, doing operations and treatments, but today will be different. I'd better get off to see Mrs Eccles now.'

'Er . . . Charlie, I was thinking . . . if you do have to put Brutus to sleep, there's this dog needing a good home very urgently or it'll have to be put down too.' She pointed to the notice on the board. 'Do you think you might be able to persuade Mrs Eccles to help out? Even if it's only till a permanent new home could be found for this dog?'

'No, I don't think it would be very tactful. The poor woman would never cope with another dog so soon. It's heartbreaking, but it can't be helped. See you later. And thanks again for all your help.'

'I've really enjoyed it. And I don't think I've caused too much chaos.'

After she'd waved him off, she went into the back room. She'd never been in there before and was fascinated by the orderliness of everything.

She pushed open another door and was greeted by a flurry of barks and miaows. There were two dogs and a couple of cats in cages. She spoke soothingly to them and they quietened.

Through another door, she found a tiny kitchen where a kettle and a jar of coffee made a welcome sight. She never had had any breakfast, she realised. She hoped the tin of biscuits wasn't a personal possession as she opened it and took out a couple.

She ate them quickly, taking two more to have with her coffee, promising that she could always replace them if necessary. She really did need her breakfast and a good dose of caffeine in the morning.

Time moved on, and she began to wonder how Charlie was getting on with Mrs Eccles. It was almost midday and there was still no sign of him coming back.

Claire, his receptionist and assistant, would have found all sorts of things to do, but Rachel was rather lost as she wandered around, looking for tasks.

At last she saw his Range Rover draw up outside and went to greet him.

'What happened?' she asked him as soon as he got out of the car. He looked drawn and rather pale.

'It was horrible. The poor dog was in

a dreadful state, but she seemed to think there must be something I could do. There really was only one thing and she couldn't accept it. I spent about an hour trying to comfort her and persuade her it was the only solution.'

'And did she agree?'

'Finally. I've just taken him to the pet cemetery for her. The awful thing is that now I have to send her a bill for doing something she desperately didn't want to have done.'

'Poor you.' She gave him a hug. 'It's a horrid part of your work. But essential. You're such a kind person, I expect you were lovely with Mrs Eccles. I suppose she wouldn't take this other dog?'

'I didn't ask her. Think about it, Rachel. She's grieving over Brutus. Another dog would be like rubbing salt into the wound.'

'OK. It was just an idea. Now, do you want coffee? I'm afraid I helped myself to the biscuits.'

'Good. I never did give you break-fast.' He glanced at his watch. 'I've just got time for a quick cuppa and then I must get on. I've several animals to check on. If they're all right then you can phone their owners to come and collect them.'

'There are several more phone messages, and some orders for repeat prescriptions that I wasn't sure about. I said they could be collected at the afternoon surgery. I hope that was all right?'

'You've done brilliantly. Thank you so much for stepping in. I doubt if Claire will be back tomorrow, so if you're free, do you think you could come again? If not, it won't matter so much because Michelle, my nurse, will be here, but we do have various ops scheduled — two kittens to be spayed and a dog whose teeth are giving problems. Then there are a couple of other things I can't even remember without looking them up. I prefer not to put people off if I can help it. They've probably worked themselves up into a state about their pets. So, what do you say?'

'I've enjoyed it. I'm sure tomorrow won't be a problem. Don't you want me any more today?'

'Well, if you're offering, could you come back for the afternoon surgery session? It's four till six.'

'Great. OK. I'll stay and make those phone calls for you, then I'll go and get an enormous lunch . . . to make up for missing breakfast.'

'Tell you what, I'll buy you lunch at the café down the road.'

'What, our rivals?'

'I was thinking of Maisie's place. Pie and chips or something. If your mum did lunches, I'd be in your place every day. No contest.'

'You're on. You owe me! Now, go and check on your patients. There's one dog ready to leap out of its cage if it doesn't get released from its prison soon.'

Half an hour later, she had made the calls to the various owners and arranged for them to come to collect their pets later in the day.

Once the prescriptions were all ready

for collection, they crossed the road to the little café.

'Hello, Rachel. Don't often see you in here. Everything all right at home?' asked Maisie.

Her real name was Sarah but the previous owner of the café had been called Maisie and so she had inherited the name along with the business.

'I'm here as payment for standing in as Charlie's receptionist.' Rachel laughed. 'But everyone's fine at home. Just don't let on you've seen me here or Mum will have a fit.'

'Is the new craft centre affecting your business much? I know *we've* seen a drop in lunch-time trade. I reckon it's the convenient parking as much as anything. People who are stopping off there on their way to St Truan are having a meal while they're at it. Bit worrying, really.'

'We've been affected, too.'

'Do you know who owns the place?'

'Can't seem to find out.'

'Do you know, Charlie?' Maisie asked.

Charlie just gave a non-committal shrug and ordered his meal.

'That was great,' Rachel said as she cleared her plate. 'Just what I needed. Thanks. Now, if you don't mind, I'll pop back to the shop for a while — make sure they're managing without me and let them know my plans for later. I dashed out so fast this morning, I barely spoke to Mum and Dad. See you later.'

* * *

The afternoon clinic seemed much busier than the one in the morning and Rachel was kept on the go the whole time, organising the clients and their pets.

One dog disgraced itself and she had to go through to the back room to look for a mop and bucket and disinfectant. Clearly it was a frequent event as everything was to hand.

She spent some time petting a tiny puppy that was there to have its inoculations and decided there was definitely an up side to being a vet.

At one point, she looked up to see a hamster cage sitting on her desk and a small child lurking behind it.

'Please, miss,' said a little voice. 'Please, miss, my hamster's foot's bleeding and my mum said I had to bring him here. But I haven't got any money.'

'Go and sit down and I'll speak to Mr Williams about it and we'll see what we can do.'

'He's called Carroty 'cos he's sort of carroty coloured.'

'Right, well, I'll see if we can help Carroty.'

When the next patient came out, she went in to ask Charlie what to do.

'I know this one. The mother always sends the kid in on his own so she doesn't have to pay, although I always try to let children's pets have free treatment for minor ailments anyway. There are a few pensioners whose pets I try to look after, too. So of course I'll see the little thing. But he must take his turn.'

'There's a side to you I don't even know about, Charlie Williams. That's a really nice gesture.'

The child was delighted when told he could wait and that the vet would see his beloved hamster.

The other people waiting smiled, too.

'Nice young man, isn't he?' Rachel commented happily.

At last the final patient had left, all the prescriptions had been handed out, and the hospitalised pets had gone home. Carroty had been diagnosed with a ripped toenail and Charlie had clipped and sprayed the claw with an antiseptic and sent it and its small owner home.

'There will be a few early clients tomorrow. Animals that are to have operations are usually brought in by their owners before breakfast. That way they won't be looked at by indignant brown eyes because their pets haven't been fed. So I'll be here anyway, but if you come when you can, that would be great.'

'No problem. At this rate I might even be looking for a permanent job here. Especially if my parents are forced out of business.'

'Surely it wouldn't come to that?'

'Who knows? Well, I'll see you tomorrow.'

'I'll pay you the going rate, of course. You won't have to work for nothing.'

'Don't worry, I'm pleased to help. You'll still have to pay Claire, won't you? You probably need to conserve all the profits you can.'

'Well, there are loads of new pieces of equipment on the market that I'd like to invest in. It took me months to persuade Dad that we needed the ultrasound. But it's been invaluable. I'd like to upgrade and be able to offer much more of a service to patients. Still, that's all in the future. Thanks again for today.'

★ ★ ★

Rachel ended up working with Charlie for the rest of the week. She loved the job, and being with him for most of the day was an added bonus. She admired his professionalism and his kindness to both people and animals.

The only black spot was when the woman who was moving home brought her mongrel in to be put down. There had been no offers of a home for it and she was forced to accept the end even though it was heartbreaking.

Almost in tears herself, Rachel took the dog through to the kennels and put it in a pen, planning to ask Charlie if there was any more they could do to find it a home. She promised the distraught owner that she would try to work something out and, taking an awful chance, she decided to call Mrs Eccles herself and ask how she was coping.

'That's really sweet of you, dear. Thank you for your concern. The house is so empty and I'm feeling really lonely without poor dear Brutus.'

'I know this is probably an impertinence on my part, but I'm wondering if you might be able to help me with a problem. I have a dog here who will have to be put down unless I can find her a home. She's a very sweet animal. She's only five and has a lot of time ahead of her if I can only find someone to look after her.'

'Oh, I'm not sure. Suppose we don't get on together?'

'Then perhaps you could give her a temporary home until I can find somewhere else? I could bring her round this afternoon for you to meet her, if you like?'

'Well, all right. I don't like to think of her being put down, and if it would help you out. Mr Williams has always been so good to me. I'll see you later then, dear. It was nice of you to think of me.'

However, when Rachel told Charlie what she had arranged, he was furious, accusing her of being unethical and interfering while she protested that it solved problems all round.

'But why were you phoning Mrs Eccles in the first place? It makes it very difficult if that's what people expect from us in the future.'

'I'm sorry, but it's a lovely dog and this could be a perfect solution. If it's the cost of the call you're worried about, I'll pay for it myself.'

'Don't be ridiculous. It does seem as if it might work out so you're forgiven — but you might just be too soft-hearted to work here much longer.'

He put his arms round her and kissed her and she felt fully forgiven.

★ ★ ★

Rachel described her day to her mother when she returned home.

'It's so nice to be working with Charlie. And doing this sort of work is so rewarding. I don't think he was too pleased with my interference, but Mrs Eccles was quite enchanted by Mitzi when they met. I think it's a match made in heaven. I'm not even going to try to look for another home for the dog. Mrs Eccles is going to phone early next week to say how the two of them are getting on.'

'So you'll be back to working with boring old antiques next week,' her mother commented.

'I love it here, Mum! I've got no regrets at all about my decision to come back. I'm just so lucky to have such a welcoming home to come back to.'

Her mother smiled and gave her a hug.

* * *

Easter came and went and the little shop began to get busier. Several times Audrey had to bake extra scones during the day as supplies ran out by mid-afternoon.

Rachel had even managed to persuade her parents to let her make some small improvements to the premises. Extra lighting and new shelving and table covers had brightened the place up a little.

'Guess what?' her father said one morning as he came into the shop. 'Those Cornwall Developments people who own the craft centre have made another offer for our place. They've upped it by a measly few thousand pounds, 'in view of your increased trade lately,' they say. The cheek of them! They must have a spy around here, looking to see how we're doing.'

'I hope you'll give them the same answer as before,' said Rachel. 'I'll write another letter, will I?'

'Maybe that really is all this place is worth,' Audrey said doubtfully.

'Nonsense. A prime site like this?'

*   *   *

A few days later, they were horrified to look out of the shop window and find it partially obscured by a huge new sign.

'What on earth is that?' Audrey gasped.

They all went outside to discover that, firmly concreted into the side of the grass verge, was a bright-red and yellow sign advertising *The Antiques and Craft Centre . . . one mile ahead.* In smaller letters, the sign listed the various facilities available at the centre, including *Traditional cream teas, pasties and light lunches.*

'How on earth did they get planning permission for this and why weren't we given the chance to object?' Jack said angrily. 'I'll get on to the council right away.'

'Who's going to come into our place if they see that sign? Oh, dear, it looks as if we might have to accept that offer after all,' wailed Audrey.

A Shocking Discovery

'It's all part of the same process of intimidation,' Rachel said angrily. 'I'm determined to find out who's behind all this. Cornwall Developments indeed. You phone about that hideous sign, Dad, and I'll write a stroppy letter to this bunch of con artists. That sign spoils the whole village. They must have put it there without permission.'

The Cranhams were not the only people to complain. When Jack finally got through to the council planning department, they said that they'd been inundated with calls all morning. As far as the council knew, there had been notification in the press about the erection of the sign, and notices had been sent to any people who might be affected by it. The period for objections had passed without anyone complaining and so permission had been granted.

'But have you any idea what it looks like? And it blocks off half our shop window. We were certainly never notified of the application. And from what you say, most of the village would have objected if they'd known about it beforehand. I've got a good mind to take an axe to it.'

The planners were not impressed with that idea and said they would visit the site to inspect it as soon as possible.

'Honestly,' Jack stormed. 'I've never heard the like. It's a gigantic con from start to finish. I thought they were obliged to send personal letters to anyone involved?'

'Calm down, dear. If you get upset like that, you'll make yourself ill.'

'They're trying to sabotage our business so they can buy it for peanuts. Rachel's right. They're not getting our shop for next to nothing. They'll pay through the nose for it if they want it that badly. It's not even as though we're competition for them. It's the other way round, if you ask me.'

It was two days before the planning officer called. He had a folder containing all the relevant papers, including copies of the letters he said had been sent to every business in the High Street. But since it appeared that nobody had actually received one, he suspected that there must have been a clerical error.

'A deliberate one, perhaps?' Jack suggested. 'Could someone have been given a back-hander to keep it quiet?'

'I hope you'll take back that accusation, sir,' the planner said brusquely. 'There has clearly been some sort of mistake and it will be investigated as soon as possible. Meantime, I trust there will be no damage caused to this sign. I do admit, it's pretty horrible, and we'll take steps to have it removed as soon as possible. Its not at all in keeping with this picturesque village. I'm certain there have been discrepancies between the planning submission and the final result. We'd never have passed this.'

Two weeks later, the sign was still there and Jack gritted his teeth each time he looked at it. Their trade had indeed suffered. Most of the other traders in the village felt the same way that Jack and Audrey did and couldn't wait to see it removed. Someone suggested a can of spray paint might help, but they were largely a law-abiding lot and the sign remained in all its lurid glory.

Rachel and Charlie continued to see a lot of each other. They often went to the cinema when he had evenings off and had also been to several concerts around the county.

Rachel had also found the time to meet up with some of her old friends.

Chloe and Mike invited her over to dinner one evening and asked if she wanted to bring someone. When she said she would bring Charlie, Chloe gave a whoop.

'That's really great. I knew you two should be together. Now, have you got anything more to tell me? Plans of any sort that I should know about?'

Rachel put her right on that score!

Why was it that, when a couple went out together for more than two dates, everyone started assuming wedding bells would ring at any moment?

It was nice, though, to be considered a couple. On some occasions when there was an emergency call-out, she accompanied Charlie and began to learn more about his work. She began to recognise horses suffering from laminitis, the painful swelling of a foot joint. She asked what caused it.

'It's usually because of too much rich grass, but there are other possible causes. You just have to look around and see what might be aggravating it. Then it's a strict diet and restricted movement. Horses that are used to being outside hate it when they're confined to a stable.'

'You have to know about every kind of animal to be a vet, don't you? Everything from horses to hamsters.'

'That's about it for a country vet. But I love it. There's no chance of getting bored. I sometimes think I need a partner, though. Dad's not really up to it any more. I'm thinking of taking on a student for a year's experience. He or she would have to be supervised but at least I could have help with the routine stuff, vaccinations and so on. Trouble is, they'd need accommodation, and everywhere's so expensive these days.'

'Hmm . . . ' mused Rachel. They were in Charlie's apartment drinking coffee and she carried her mug over to the window and looked out.

'You could always put a caravan in the garden,' she suggested.

'Hey, there's an idea. Actually, I think the old stable might be a better idea. I'll get my cousin to look at it. It might convert to another apartment.'

'Your cousin?'

'He's a builder. Well, he used to be. He calls himself a property developer these days.'

Alarm bells rang in Rachel's head.

'And what's his company's name?' she asked, though somehow she knew what the answer was going to be.

'Cornwall Developments.'

'I don't believe it! Charlie, that's the company behind the Antiques and Craft Centre!'

'Well, yes. I always meant to tell you but everyone seemed so angry about it.'

'I wonder why?' she said with heavy sarcasm. 'Do you know they've been trying to buy our shop at a ludicrously low price? And now they've put up this awful sign, obviously designed to put us right out of business. They even cheated the planners with that one. But it isn't staying. If they don't remove it legally, I shall personally take my father's axe to it.'

'I'm sorry. I admit I should have told you about it, but . . . '

Rachel couldn't believe that he didn't seem to find any of this important; that all the worry and distress that her parents had been subjected to didn't matter.

'Like you said, we were all very angry about it and still are. In fact, Charlie, I'm so angry that I don't think I want to be associated with someone whose family could do this to us — and to the whole village.'

'It isn't me, Rachel, it's my cousin. If you must know, we don't really get on. I certainly would never approve of his business methods.' He gave a sarcastic laugh. 'No wonder he's so successful. He's already built loads of new houses and flats around the area, despite all manner of opposition.'

'But you knew about it! I asked you several times if you knew who was behind the craft centre. Even Maisie asked you in the café. And don't try to pretend you knew nothing about any of this at the time. I simply don't believe you. Goodbye, Charlie. I'm sorry, but we're finished.'

'Rachel . . . you're overreacting. Geoff's nothing to do with me. Well, not really.'

'Goodbye, Charlie.' She flung open the door and stormed out of his apartment which had become so familiar to her.

Tearfully she walked back to her own home. She would miss seeing him, and had lost the future she had been dreaming of.

She went into the living-room and slumped down in the armchair.

'Hello, love. You want some cocoa? Dad's just made some ... Oh, my goodness, just look at your face. What on earth's happened?'

'I've just discovered who's the driving force behind Cornwall Developments. It's Charlie's cousin. And Charlie knew all the time. No wonder he looked so uneasy every time we mentioned the new Antiques and Craft Centre! So I've finished with him. I couldn't carry on seeing someone who could be such a liar. How would I ever trust him again?'

'That seems a bit harsh. It's hardly his fault.'

'But he knows how worried we are about the new place and he never once mentioned that he knows who it belongs to, let alone that it's owned by a member of his family. Well, at least I know now who we're fighting. And believe me, Cornwall Developments have a fight on their hands.'

★ ★ ★

For the next few weeks, Rachel frantically scanned planning applications to discover exactly how many building projects Cornwall Developments were involved with.

'Do you know who actually bought Auntie Marjorie's house?'

'No idea. The estate agent just told her there had been an offer at the asking price and she took it. She didn't really want to think about it too much. You know how she was about all her china and things.'

'I bet we can guess who it was. I'm going to look and see if there are any planning application notices up.'

She walked round to Marjorie's old house which looked a bit sad now it was empty. Sure enough, there was a yellow planning application notice pinned to the gate.

Proposed demolition of existing house with request for planning for six architect-designed houses to be built on adjoining land with provision for two starter homes in line with local requirements.

'I knew it,' she muttered.

She kept on with her research and what she discovered made interesting reading. Charlie's cousin's company was getting approval for developments all over the county because they always included starter homes for local people in their projects. It was a winning formula. Most people in the area were up in arms over the lack of affordable homes for young people, who were forced to leave the county when they couldn't find a place to suit their budget.

She fully approved of the idea of affordable housing, of course, but for every starter home that he built, Geoff was also building a dozen executive-style places, probably for rich people to buy as second homes.

He also seemed to have a reputation for cramming too many unsightly buildings into small spaces.

She went to look at some of these and was shocked at the way several flats were crammed into a space where one older house had once stood.

Then she discovered that there were at least three sites in her own village for which planning applications had been submitted by Cornwall Developments. It seemed that every bit of land that was ever up for sale was being snapped up by Geoff's consortium. The whole character of St Truan, and many of its surrounding villages, was coming increasingly under threat from these new developments.

'You know what? I reckon he wants to build several flats on the site of our shop. If he can get it at — literally — a knock-down price, and puts up a block of four or six apartments in its place, just think of the profit he'll rake in.'

'And think what it would do to our little cottage. Why, we'd be stuck down the drive with no outlook at all. Just brick walls to look at.'

'They'd never get permission for that surely?' Jack protested.

'Don't bank on it. He's already got permission for all manner of things. Whatever the council says, he definitely knows which strings to pull to get what he wants.

'If there are dozens of new blocks of flats and houses built in this village, not only will it ruin the look of the place, but where will the children go to school? And how will the doctors cope? And what about jobs? Where on earth will that number of extra people find work? I'm going to organise a village meeting. He won't ruin St Truan. I won't let him.'

She went upstairs and switched on her laptop. Organising a campaign was what she could do best. It was what she was trained for. It might not be quite her usual sort of advertising campaign, but the process couldn't be that different. She began to design posters and flyers.

Downstairs, her parents were considering her plans.

'I just wish we could be shot of all of it. Do you think we shall ever get a decent offer? I know we've been complaining about trade being slow, but I'm almost dreading the influx of summer visitors and the work that means.'

'I know, love. But we have to support Rachel, and, anyway, we don't want to see the village ruined, do we?'

'All the same, I haven't got the energy for this. Not at my time of life.'

* * *

Rachel worked hard at raising support for her meeting. There were a number of local people who had been approached by Cornwall Developments, all being offered low prices for their property.

Everyone she approached agreed to

put up posters and to hand out flyers and she had to make a trip to buy more ink for her printer.

She contacted the local press and radio and was interviewed several times, making impassioned speeches about the need for change but in a sensitive way.

She saw nothing of Charlie, and if he was even aware of her campaign, he was making no comment. She missed him and felt sad to think of the reason why her hopes and dreams of a future with him had been wiped out.

She tried giving all her thoughts and energy to the campaign, but it didn't entirely work, although she did manage to tire herself out and fall into bed exhausted most evenings.

But always she'd keep thinking of something he'd said or somewhere they'd been together.

'You *are* both coming to the meeting on Thursday, aren't you?' she asked her parents.

'Well, actually, love, we'd rather not.'

Audrey looked anxiously at her daughter as she spoke.

'But, Mum, you can't let me down.'

'The thing is, Rachel, your mum and I — well, we're ready to retire. If we're honest, we were about to tell you we were putting the house and shop on the market when you arrived home.'

'I can't believe it. You want to retire?'

She felt the blood draining from her face and her head felt light and dizzy. The real truth was dawning on her.

'Yes. I want a nice little bungalow. No stairs to climb a hundred times a day. No dusty nooks and crannies to keep clean.'

'And I ruined it all for you! I blundered in like a tank to take over all your plans without thinking. Oh, Mum — Dad — I'm so sorry. I thought you'd be so pleased to have me back home and helping out. And all the time, you've been wishing I'd disappear back to London. No wonder you were hoping to marry me off to Charlie. I promise, I'll find a job and move away as soon as I can.'

'No, Rachel! Don't be silly! We don't want to get rid of you, of course not. We're delighted to have you home again. It's just that the timing was a bit off. It had taken us a long time to reach our decision and we were about to tell you when you made us think again. There's no question of us turning you out. We just don't want to be a part of your protests and meetings. But I think you're doing the right thing and we admire you for sticking up for your principles.'

'Looks like we all have quite a lot of planning to think about. Maybe this time next year we shall all look back and wonder what all the fuss was about. You in your easy-to-run bungalow and me . . . well, who knows where?'

Everything seemed up in the air and they all felt rather unsettled.

★ ★ ★

Rachel came downstairs the next morning to find Binkie curled up and

271

refusing to move. The cat was clearly in pain and miaowed pitifully when Rachel tried to pick her up.

'Come on, old girl. There's your milk. Don't you want it?' Rachel stroked the cat gently. 'What do you think is wrong?' she asked her mother.

'I really don't know. She'll have to be taken to see Charlie, I'm afraid. Could you . . . I mean, would you be willing to take her?'

'Oh, Mum, I don't know. I'm not sure I can face him.'

'You'll have to one day. You can't avoid him for ever in a small village like this.'

'You're right. And we're both adults, after all. OK, I'll take her. Poor old thing, aren't you?'

After breakfast, she put the cat in the pet carrier and walked along the street to the vet's. She pushed open the waiting-room door and booked in at reception.

Waiting her turn, she was a bundle of nerves. She tried telling herself that it was only Charlie that she was about to face. Her own, dear Charlie, whom she could no longer allow herself to love.

Her name was called and then she was face to face with him.

'There's something wrong with Binkie.' Her voice faltered slightly as she spoke to the man she knew she would always love.

'Let's have a look, then. Clearly something's wrong . . . she isn't even spitting and hissing at me. Come on, old girl. What is it, eh?'

He lifted Binkie out and she lay still on the table. A small miaow came from her throat. Expertly, he felt along her tummy and looked into her mouth.

'I think I need to do an X-ray. She'll need sedating, of course. Has she eaten or drunk anything today?'

'Nothing since last night. And she didn't eat much then, now that I think about it.'

Rachel's voice was trembling slightly and her heart felt as if it was beating in her throat. However, Charlie was concentrating on the cat and seemed unaware of her.

'I'll give her an injection. I assume you're aware that this might not help much? She is an old cat and sometimes anaesthetics can cause respiratory problems.'

'Yes, of course. But she's clearly suffering and she can't be left like that.'

Charlie nodded approvingly.

'OK. I'll just take her through. If you'd like to wait outside, I'll let you know when she's had the X-ray. I'll leave her with the nurse for a while until I finish up here. Actually, if you want to go home, I'll get someone to call you when we know more.'

'I'd rather wait, if that's all right. Mum would hate it if I went back without Binkie and without knowing the problem . . .'

'Fine.' He picked up the cat and went towards the rear door of the consulting room. Then he stopped and looked back at her.

'Rachel, we need to talk.'

'There's nothing more to say. You know my feelings.'

'But you're being so unfair. Please? I'm begging you. You must listen to my side of things. I still love you. I miss you and I want us to be together. This is all a huge misunderstanding.'

'I can't. I daren't. Besides, I might be going back to London.'

'But you said you couldn't live anywhere else but Cornwall!'

'I was being foolish. I can live wherever I want to.'

'Come out with me this evening and let's talk this through. Please?'

She promised to think about it while she was waiting for Binkie.

She sat down in the waiting-room and watched one cat and two dogs come and go for treatment. They were the last patients.

It seemed to take an eternity for Charlie to come to tell her what was happening. Her mum would be so upset if there was something seriously wrong with the cat. Suppose Binkie never woke up again? But she had confidence in Charlie — even if he had told lies to her about his cousin's involvement in the village.

She thought about that. Had he actually told any lies? She couldn't remember. Her grievances were much more centred on the fact that he knew all about the craft centre and hadn't told her. It was more that he had lied by omission. Maybe she *should* give him the chance to tell his side of the story.

At last he came through to the waiting-room.

'She needs an operation. She has a small hernia but it's causing her a lot of discomfort. I can do it right away if you like, while she's still anaesthetised. You should call your mother and ask if it's what she wants.'

'It'll be all right. I mean, she'll want whatever's best for Binkie. I'll tell her what's happening when I get back.'

'Right. Well, I'll get to it then and give you a call when it's over. No point in your waiting around. I'll want to keep her at least overnight.' He turned to go back to his operating room, but again stopped in the doorway. 'Did you have time to think? About us.'

'Yes. I'll see you this evening if you've time . . . just to talk.'

'We'll have a meal. No, I insist — I haven't had time for lunch.'

Audrey was most upset when Rachel told her the news about Binkie.

'Poor old cat. I should have realised something was wrong, but because we've all been feeling so unsettled, I didn't take much notice of her. Poor little thing.'

'Don't worry. Charlie seems to think it isn't too serious. And as she'd already had a sedative, it means she doesn't have to have two lots of anaesthetic. That's the difficult part for an elderly animal.'

★　★　★

It was a couple of hours before the phone rang. It was Charlie's receptionist saying that all was well. The operation had been a success but the cat would need to stay in overnight. The vet apologised for not calling personally but he'd had to go out to an emergency.

'Thanks very much, dear,' Audrey said as she put down the phone. 'Binkie's all right,' she said rather unnecessarily. 'He's a good vet but, my word, he does have to work hard.'

'Then maybe he won't be free this evening after all,' Rachel remarked.

Audrey's eyes lit up. 'Oh, why do you mention that?'

'He wants to put his side of things and I've agreed to meet him and listen to what he has to say.'

'Thank goodness for that! I'm sick of you moping around like a misery.'

'I have not been moping around. I've been working very hard,' she protested.

'Well, you have to admit you've been very quiet lately. That always was a sign that you were moping about something.'

'Sorry. It's so difficult to know what to do. I mean, he refused to say anything when I asked him if he knew. I've been trying to think if he actually lied about not knowing what was going on with Cornwall Developments. I don't think he did, but it was as good as lying, wasn't it?'

'I like Charlie,' was her mother's only comment.

'I like Charlie too, but what am I supposed to do? If he can lie about this, how can I ever really trust him?'

'I'm sorry, Rachel, but it's up to you. You're a grown woman now and I'm certainly not making this sort of decision for you. If you see him tonight, then you'll just have to decide for yourself what you want to do and how you feel.'

Passionate Meetings

At seven o'clock that evening, Charlie called Rachel on her mobile. 'I'm running a bit late but I've booked a table for dinner at Leward Cove. It's usually nice and quiet there and we should be able to talk without the waitress coming to ask if we want any sauce.'

Rachel laughed at the memory.

'I'll be with you by quarter to eight,' he told her.

'OK, I'll be ready.'

She was still unsure if she was wise to go out with him but it was such a silly situation.

On impulse, she decided to wear the long skirt and jacket she had bought for Chloe's wedding. He'd liked her in it, he'd said it suited her — and it was quite a smart restaurant they were going to.

'You look swish,' Jack commented. 'Special occasion?'

'Not really. This is a confidence booster, I guess.'

'Have a nice time.'

She went outside and realised what a lovely evening it was. They would probably be able to watch the sun setting on the water if they hurried.

And the dreaded sign had disappeared! There were two patches of rubble on the verge where it had stood. She wondered who had removed it but didn't really care that much. She was just delighted it had gone.

Charlie's Range Rover appeared along the street and she stepped forward as he pulled in at the kerb.

'Sorry I'm late. Wow, you look pretty special. Thank you for taking the trouble.'

He held out a hand to assist her into the vehicle but she avoided it and managed on her own. His face fell. She noticed that he too had dressed carefully, in a suit, and she wondered why. He usually wore smartish jeans and a sweater or T-shirt to take her out, but it was nice to dress up and go to a more stylish restaurant.

'You looking pretty smart, too,' she remarked. 'Any reason?'

'Just the fact that you've agreed to spend time with me. By the way, did you get the message about Binkie? She came through pretty well.'

'Yes, thanks. Your receptionist said you were called out again?'

'Yes. No rest for the wicked. Sick sheep this time. I can't complain about a lack of variety.'

The conversation was somewhat stilted as they were both obviously tense.

'Not much further,' he said fatuously as he drove along.

'No,' she agreed.

They stopped in the little car park. Theirs was the only vehicle.

'Quiet night.'

'Looks like it.'

They went inside and were shown to

a table near the window and given the menus.

'Just mineral water, please,' she ordered. They would probably have wine with the meal and she wanted to keep a clear head.

Charlie ordered the same.

She concentrated on the menu, postponing the moment when they had to talk properly. How had things turned so sour?

'I wonder how many times we've sat opposite each other over a meal in the past few months? Seems we're always eating or drinking.'

'It's somewhere we can be on our own. I always did think meals should be sociable affairs rather than pure nutrition,' Charlie replied with a grin. 'Though the fact that I love food might have something to do with it! Your Mum's a fantastic cook. I'm not sure about you. Do you get to do a lot of cooking?'

'No. I quite like to cook, but I rarely get to use the kitchen when Mum's around. Charlie, I . . . '

'Hush. I have something to say first and we'll get to explanations later.'

'Are you ready to order?' the waiter asked as he placed their mineral water in front of them.

Rachel nodded. She had chosen a chicken dish and Charlie went for his favourite fish.

The waiter gave the hint of a bow as he left the table.

'I have to ask you something, Rachel. Do you still love me or have I completely blown it?'

'I do love you, Charlie, but . . . '

'I don't want to hear any buts. Please let me have my say. I know how badly I've treated you, believe me. I was out of mind *not* to see it. I really don't deserve the way you've stuck by me with such amazing loyalty. I can't think why I was so weak-minded over Gemma all those months. It's quite out of character for me to be so wishy-washy about making decisions.

'I think I always knew deep inside

that it was never going to work between us and I should have acknowledged that. Then you came back into my life like a whirlwind. I'm hoping I haven't left it too late for us. Once you *had* come back into my life, I should have realised right away that you were the only woman for me. Rachel, what I'm trying to say is, I love you and . . . will you marry me?'

She gasped at the sheer unexpectedness of it. She had been staring at him intently throughout his speech, wondering till the very last moment what was coming.

Before she could reply, he was pulling something from his pocket.

He held out a tiny box, and when she opened it, she saw an exquisite diamond ring. It was set in platinum and couldn't have been more perfect if she had chosen it herself.

She dragged her gaze away from it and looked into Charlie's brilliant-blue eyes. He looked so anxious, so wonderful.

She held out a hand to take his and smiled. She didn't need to give his proposal more than a moment's consideration.

'Yes, please,' she whispered.

'Oh, thank heavens! I was so sure I'd blown it with you for ever.'

He took her hand and kissed her fingers.

'Darling Rachel. I love you so much.'

He turned and signalled to the waiter who was hovering in the background with a bottle of champagne, then he slipped the ring on to her finger.

Of course it was a perfect fit, exactly as she might have expected on this magical night.

'But you're not entirely off the hook,' she told him. 'I'm still furious and disappointed that you knew about your cousin's involvement with the craft centre and didn't tell me. And I'm organising a campaign against unsuitable building projects in the village.'

'I could hardly miss it. Everywhere I go there are posters or flyers and lots of angry people. I trust you noticed that the sign's gone from outside your shop?'

'Yes, I did. But when did it go? And who took it down?'

'I'm afraid I'm the guilty party. I tackled Geoff about it and he just grinned and said it was tough. All in the name of competition or something like that. I got a little mad and he said I could take it down if I wanted to. It had served its purpose. It's dumped behind your shop actually, but at least it's out of sight. I thought it might make a nice bonfire at some point.'

She laughed. At least he was on her side at last.

The food arrived and they ate hungrily.

'I hope I can rely on you to help with the campaign?' she asked, wondering how far his loyalties could be stretched.

'Of course. I can understand why you need to fight for your business and want to protest against this mass of building projects. Besides, it's in my own interest to keep in favour with everyone in the village. After all, most of my customers live here, don't they? Mind you, a few more houses might mean a few more pets needing looked after.'

'Charlie Williams, don't you dare tease me!'

'Maybe we shall manage that meal with my parents now. The last one was cancelled after you dumped me so unceremoniously. They'll have to feed my fiancée, now that I have one, won't they?'

'I'll need to get used to that title. I remember Chloe saying the same thing before the wedding. Maybe we'll be able to go to Chloe and Mike's for that dinner invitation that also got lost during our difficulties.'

'Seems to me that we're logging up quite a few free meals here. So, tell me, what's next?'

'I suppose it's the meeting. The idea is to make sure everyone is fully informed about the building proposals.

If they disagree that they must be stopped, they'll be able to vote against making a formal protest. Somehow I don't think too many people are going to disagree. Most people are happy with some development, but not on the scale your cousin is proposing.'

'Rachel?' Charlie interrupted.

'Yes?'

'When I asked what was next, I meant for us! I mean, is this going to be a long engagement or can I expect to have a wife in the near future?'

'Oh, I see. Sorry.' She paused and thought for a moment.

'I don't know. What do you think?'

'I can't see any reason to wait for too long. Next week would do for me.'

'Next week?' she squealed. 'Now I know you're crazy. You clearly have no idea of how much organisation a wedding entails.'

'I hope we don't have to have a massive affair like Chloe's. It was very nice but not really me — us, rather.'

'Well, let's not rush things. Let's get

used to being engaged first. I'll have to have time to get used to calling you my fiancé for starters.' She looked down at her finger. 'This ring is just perfect. I love it.'

'I'm glad. How about going back to tell your parents now? Have coffee there instead of here?'

'If you like. I'm not sure how they'll take it — though if it's any consolation to you, when I said I was going out tonight, Mum said she really likes you.'

He grinned his lovely, boyish grin that melted her heart completely, just as it always had done.

'Then I've got my feet under the table right away, haven't I?'

★   ★   ★

Rachel's parents were reaching the 'last cup of cocoa' time and were rather surprised when Charlie and Rachel came in together.

'We've got some news,' Rachel burst out. 'Look.' She held out her hand to show them her ring.

'What the . . . ? Oh, my dears. I'm so thrilled! Delighted! Oh, Charlie, I'm — well, pleased as punch.'

'I think he gathered that, Mum.'

'It's all bit sudden, though, isn't it?' her father asked.

'Well, maybe,' Rachel admitted with a grin. 'Actually, it was the only way I could get him on our side for the protest meeting,' she added wickedly.

Her father laughed.

'We should open a bottle of something,' he suggested.

'Another time, if you don't mind.' Charlie smiled and said he needed to go and check that Binkie was all right.

'What, you mean she's been left on her own all evening?' Audrey said in horror.

Charlie smiled. 'She would have slept almost the entire time. She's safe in one of our sterile cage kennels and we're sure she can't hurt herself. But I always check on our overnight guests before I leave them. You should be able to collect her tomorrow, around lunchtime if all's well. I'll monitor her during the morning and I'll call you to let you know how she is. So, I'll say goodnight to you now.'

'We're really delighted, Charlie. Welcome to the family.' Jack was looking quite emotional.

'Goodnight, fiancé,' Rachel said. 'And thank you for a wonderful evening. It was all most unexpected and certainly not what I would ever have dreamed could happen when I got up this morning.'

'Goodnight, my love. And thank you for saying yes.'

'Come and tell us all about it,' Audrey demanded after Charlie had gone. 'Did you perhaps have a hint of what was coming when you went out all dressed up?'

'Not a clue. But it all feels so right. Charlie's everything I could want in a husband. Oh, heavens, that all sounds so very grown up doesn't it?'

'It's about time you settled down.

You're not getting any younger and nor are we. We'll be too old to enjoy our grandchildren if you leave it much longer.'

'Mu-um! We've just got engaged and haven't even decided on a wedding date yet. Now you've got us with a tribe of little ones for you to spoil.'

'Sorry. But it's important. We must begin planning the wedding very soon. Perhaps we should invite Mr and Mrs Williams round for dinner to talk it through. It would be nice to have the reception at the hotel you went to for Chloe's wedding, but I'm afraid it would be much more than we could afford. Mind you, we're probably too late for that anyway. You have to book months in advance to get in there, so I believe.'

'I think you'd better slow down, love,' Jack told her. 'Wait to see what Charlie and Rachel want. After all, they might want to wait for a while.'

'We haven't even had time to talk about it yet. We want to enjoy being engaged first. Just be satisfied that you got your way and found someone to marry me off to! I must go to bed now and try to get some sleep. I've got a lot to do in the next couple of days.'

⋆　⋆　⋆

Everything was such a rush during the next two days, what with the meeting to organise and making sure there were enough handouts for everyone who'd said they would attend. Representatives from the planning authority had said they would be there and, trying to be fair, Charlie had been asked to invite his cousin.

Secretly everyone hoped he would refuse to attend. It would be very awkward if he was there, but Rachel had to admit that she was also quite intrigued to see what he was like.

Her parents felt guilty about not participating in the actual meeting and at the last minute decided it was important to 'Save Our Village' as the campaign had been called.

They went along to the village hall and were met with a barrage of congratulations and nice comments about Rachel's engagement, and also about her tireless efforts to bring the potential building problems to everyone's attention.

Audrey and Jack were pleased they'd made the effort to come. They watched as their daughter handed out information sheets and spoke to everyone who arrived at the crowded hall.

A row of chairs and a table had been placed on the stage and a definite buzz of anticipation filled the room.

The planning officer — the same official who they had met previously — arrived with a female colleague in tow. They both carried official looking folders and a huge manual which presumably contained the policy documents for the area.

Rachel shook hands with them as introductions were made and showed them to their seats on the platform.

Looking slightly disconcerted to be facing such a large audience, they sat down obediently.

There was still no sign of Charlie or his cousin.

Seven-thirty arrived and Rachel decided not to wait any longer and to start the meeting.

She rose and rapped her knuckles on the table.

'Ladies and gentlemen,' she began nervously.

She cleared her throat and wondered what on earth could have made her be so foolish as to take on the role of chairman. She should have asked the parish councillors to do it. In fact she had gone about it all the wrong way. It should have been them doing all this, not her. Embarrassed, she found the notes she had made on a series of cards, just as she had been taught to do when making a presentation at work.

'Ladies and gentlemen,' she began again. 'First of all, my thanks to you all for turning out this evening. Our thanks, too, to the representatives from the planning department for giving us their time.'

She went on to outline the problems as she saw them, and various members of the audience raised their hands wanting to add their own objections.

'We don't want the character of the village to be changed so that nobody comes to visit here for its natural charms and pretty, old buildings.'

'How will the village services cope if a hundred more people come to live here?'

'What about the school? They're already full up.'

'Would we get more doctors and another dentist?'

At last, Rachel asked if the planning officer would like to comment.

He stood up, looking ill at ease.

'First of all, let me assure you all that we're as keen as everyone else to preserve your lovely village. We don't want to allow anything to ruin it. But there are commitments we have to make. Affordable homes, for a start.'

A loud buzz of anger went around the room.

'Define affordable,' shouted someone from the back.

'Well, we all want to provide for our younger folk and give them a place where they can afford to live.'

'And jobs? Have you got ideas about providing jobs that pay enough to buy your so-called affordable housing? How will you stop the homes being sold to the rich city types who come and buy second homes?'

The questions poured out thick and fast and as soon as the planners answered, or tried to answer one, another hand was raised.

Then Rachel noticed Charlie standing at the back of the hall with an older man. He was shorter than Charlie and on the plump side. He was expensively dressed and looked very self-satisfied.

When there was a slight pause, Rachel stood up and addressed the man.

'I see we have a local property developer in the hall. Perhaps you would like to step up and answer some of our questions?'

She hoped she had jumped to the correct conclusion and that the man was indeed Geoff.

He walked slowly down the hall towards the stage and climbed up.

'My name's Geoff Halligan. Some of you may know me already.' There were murmurs from around the hall. He continued, 'I admit I have been buying up old places around the area with the intention of doing exactly what the council representatives here are saying: replacing them with affordable homes.'

'Yeah, along with homes none of us locals can afford. You're throwing up rubbish stuff for us and posh places for the rich.'

The man who had shouted out this comment was clearly angry. He muttered something about his son who had been forced to look for a job elsewhere.

'Of course I'm building a range of

properties. We don't want to end up with ghettos like some of the big estates in the cities.'

The meeting rumbled on. There were heated exchanges at times, and Rachel couldn't manage to quell occasional bouts of shouting. At last, when she felt most people had had the opportunity to speak, she turned to the representatives from the council planning department for their final comments.

'I want to assure everyone here that we shall consider all your comments very carefully,' said the man. 'My colleague has been making notes throughout the meeting and we shall take your points to the full committee when the matters arise. Rest assured, we want your village to remain as beautiful as it is. Thank you for inviting us this evening.'

When everyone had drifted away, Charlie joined Rachel and congratulated her.

'Perhaps you'd like to meet my cousin properly now?' he suggested.

'I'm not sure he'll want to meet me. After all, we're on different sides.'

Charlie shook his head and nodded towards Geoff.

'Come and meet my fiancée,' he said, looking faintly embarrassed.

'How do you do?' Geoff shook her hand. 'I've heard a lot about you. It's Gemma, isn't it? It's about time someone got this reprobate to settle down. Well done for bringing him to heel.'

Rachel felt as if her knees were giving way.

'Actually . . . ' she began.

'This is Rachel, Geoff,' Charlie put in quickly. 'Rachel Cranham. We got engaged a couple of days ago.'

'Cranham — Cranham — where've I heard that name before?'

'My parents own the shop you've been trying to buy for peanuts. The shop you're trying to put out of business with your crummy Antiques and Craft Centre — although I feel you haven't quite learned the correct definition of the word 'antique'.'

She felt Charlie's hand tighten on her arm.

'As you see, she's a passionate lady,' he said to Geoff. 'I think we'd better leave now, darling, don't you?'

He didn't want a new war to start. After all, Geoff was part of his family, however much he disliked the man.

Happy Days!

There was a sense of anti-climax for a few days after the meeting. Rachel felt almost as if she was wandering round in a dream, waiting to wake up. She even forgot to look at her auction sites, but when she did, she was delighted to discover that two of Marjorie's pieces of sculpture had sold for over two hundred pounds each. She rushed into the shop with the good news.

To her utter astonishment, the place was packed. Her mother was dashing around attending to all the customers and several people were waiting for tables to become free so they could be served afternoon tea. Many of them were locals and they pounced on Rachel as she went into the shop.

'Well done! We needed someone like you to wake us up.'

'I haven't been in here for months!

I'd no idea you had such lovely things for sale. I shall come again when it's a bit less crowded and buy something for my sister's birthday.'

Rachel fought her way to the back of the shop where her mother was rushed off her feet filling tea pots and putting out jam and cream in little dishes.

'It's gone crazy in here today.'

'You should have called me over!'

'And when did I have time for that?' she asked. 'Take that tray to table four, will you, dear? I don't know where your father's got to.'

He arrived a moment later with a couple of large containers of milk from the shop down the road.

'Completely ran out! I don't know where everyone's coming from.'

He looked delighted at being so busy.

'This is all my fault I gather,' Rachel said happily.

'Is this cup and saucer for sale?' a lady asked, indicating the china she'd been drinking from. 'Only it's exactly the same as my set at home and I've broken some of the pieces.'

'Well, I suppose we could sell it to you,' Rachel murmured. 'I'll ask Mum.'

'Thank you so much, dear. I'm glad I came. And these scones are simply delicious. This place is a real asset to the village, don't you think?' the lady asked her companion.

'Pity they weren't here to support us all through the winter,' Jack said under his breath. 'Anyone wanting the cups off the tables, they're five pounds each. Might as well make a bit of profit.'

'Dad, you're dreadful! We probably only paid a few pence each for them.'

'So? This is a business.'

The customer actually took three cups with matching saucers and didn't even wait for them to be washed.

Rachel and her parents giggled over it later.

'We'll just have to go to some more sales, won't we, Mum? Speaking of auctions, I've got some good news. You'll never guess what we got for those two sculptures of Marjorie's?'

And they couldn't. They didn't guess anywhere near the amount.

'I know what you're up to,' her father said with a laugh. 'You're making sure we can afford that posh hotel for your wedding.'

'Actually, no. We'd like to get married on the beach, if it's all the same to you.'

'Don't be ridiculous. How can you?'

'We probably can't, but it would be nice. Then I wouldn't have to be done up like a frothy meringue. I could wear white shorts or something instead.'

'And float away on a surf board, I suppose?'

'Hey, now there's an idea.'

'Stop teasing your mother. She wants an excuse to wear a proper mother-of-the-bride outfit and she's spent the entire last two days looking at hats in various magazines. Don't deprive her of the chance. You're our only daughter, after all. With things looking up so much, we can afford the best for you.'

'Let's wait and see,' replied a now

worried Rachel.

When she saw Charlie that evening, she confided her fears.

'Mum's getting totally carried away. What on earth are we going to do?'

'It's only natural. We may have to go along with it. My parents are just relieved that I'm finally going to settle down. Honestly, you'd think I was the rake of the county and approaching fifty instead of thirty.'

'You're not nearly thirty. You're only twenty-seven. Aren't you?'

'Twenty-eight this month. Hey, there's an idea: let's get married on my birthday, then I can have the best present ever. What do you think? That way, everywhere will be booked up and we can have the simple wedding we want.'

'It might just work. But only a month to get it all organised?'

'You got the village campaign organised in little more than a week.'

'This is slightly different. Besides, where would we live?'

'My apartment for now? Or perhaps you'd like to commission one of my dear cousin's starter homes?'

Laughing, she punched him.

'So, is it to be on the twenty-sixth of next month?'

'Let me think about it for a while.'

'Had long enough?' he asked after a thirty-second pause.

She laughed. 'I guess so.'

When her parents heard their decision, her mother sat down with a thump and looked quite pale.

'You aren't serious! How will we be ready in time? I think you're completely mad.'

'No, Mum. Just deliriously happy. I'm going to marry the man of my dreams.'

She grabbed both parents and whirled them round in a joyous circle until they all collapsed on to the sofa in helpless laughter.

'I'd better order the fruit for the wedding cake. Although even if I make it right away, it'll never be mature enough.'

'Match the bride then, won't it?'

A few days later, an official letter arrived from the council.

'They've turned down the planning applications for several of the plots in the village. That's such good news. *And* the plans for an extension to the craft centre. We've won round one at least.'

Rachel rushed off and printed out a new set of handouts to circulate around the village, giving the local residents a news update.

Everyone was full of congratulations and the shop was once more filled with friends and neighbours eating scones and drinking tea and coffee.

Luckily Audrey had made several extra batches of scones and — following Rachel's advice — put them in the freezer. They soon thawed out in the microwave.

That evening, they all sat down to eat together.

'We've got something to say, Rachel,' her father began in a somewhat formal way. 'We've decided that we *will* put the shop on the market now that things are looking up. It should sell as a going concern, and with your website doing so well, we think the time is right.'

'Yes, and once we know what we can get for the shop, we'll put the cottage on the market, too, and look for a nice bungalow somewhere nearby. You won't want to work here once you're married, will you?'

'Well, I suppose it isn't unexpected, but I'm not sure what else I can do. For a job, I mean.'

'But you'll probably want to start a family soon. That will keep you busy enough, and I'm sure Charlie will earn enough so you don't have to work.'

'Stop trying to organise my life, Mum! We've barely talked about the wedding, let alone having a family. I'm sure we will, but when we're good and ready.'

'Of course, love. But don't leave it too long. You don't want to end up with an only one, do you?'

'I turned out all right, didn't I?'

''Course you did love. But we'd have liked at least one more if it could have happened.'

When they met later that evening, she told Charlie about her parents' planned retirement.

'So, I'm going to have to look for a job, no matter what my mum says about me having plenty to do when we're married.'

'Meaning?'

'Oh, you know — the grandchildren thing.'

'We haven't talked about that.'

'Of course we haven't. Let's sort out the wedding first.'

'That suggests you *are* keen to have a family?'

'I suppose so. But it's something for the future.'

'That's a relief. I want kids, too, but I have so much to do first . . . building up the practice and sorting out someone to come in to help. Dad's finally realised it's all too much for him.

Actually, though, I have a suggestion to make. About you working. Claire's just handed in her notice so I'm looking for a receptionist. How would you feel about that?'

'Oh, Charlie, that would be just perfect! I loved those few days I worked with you.'

'That's fine, but there's just one thing.'

'What?'

'No snuggling up to the vet when he's in the little back kitchen. Most unprofessional.'

'Oh, and that is the usual practice, is it?'

★ ★ ★

Three weeks later, they were all in a flat spin. It was only two days to the wedding and there were a million things still to be done.

There were several potential buyers for the shop, all of whom seemed to want to look around at the most inappropriate times. Trade had remained brisk and they had even put in the special pasty oven and experienced a huge increase in locals coming in to buy them to take away for lunch. Jack was delighted with the extra revenue for very little effort.

Rachel and Charlie had won the battle for a simple wedding, and following the service in the church were planning a picnic on the beach, just as they'd hoped.

The slightly wacky suggestion had taken off and they'd been given permission for a small marquee on the shore, near the Beach Bar. The owner of the bar was willing to close his premises to the public for the afternoon and exclusively serve the wedding guests.

Because it was all so casual, they had issued lots of invitations to all their old friends to drop in for a drink and a piece of wedding cake. Audrey had held her ground and produced a huge two-tiered creation, beautifully decorated, which would look quite out of place on a table on the beach, but nobody had the heart to stop her from doing it. After all, she had been forced to make so many other compromises over the wedding arrangements. All she was hoping for now was that it didn't pour with rain or blow one of the typical Cornish gales.

'Now, have you got your going-away case packed? And did you put in plenty of sun cream? You know how you burn if you get too much sun.'

'It's all right, Mum. Don't fuss. I've got everything I need for the honeymoon.'

'I just wish I knew where you were going.'

They were keeping their destination completely secret from everyone.

'It's only a short break. We'll be back before you know it.'

'But suppose we need to contact you?'

'You can always call my mobile. I'll put it on at least once a day, so you can leave a message if need be.'

'But I'd have liked to send some

flowers for your room.'

'Bless you, Mum. Good try. Now, have you got your hat sprayed, washed and trimmed, or whatever it needs?'

'Now you're being silly.'

Jack came rushing in.

'We've had an offer for the shop. Full asking price plus stock at valuation. What do you think?'

'Oh! Dear me, I need to sit down for a minute. Oh, my! Whatever should we do? After all these years?'

'Sell it, of course, Mum. You've been moaning about it long enough.'

'I know, but now it's happening . . . I don't quite know what to think.'

Rachel and her father laughed and laughed and the three of them hugged each other.

'Truly the end of several eras,' she said.

* * *

They sat side by side watching the sun set over the sea. 'Hasn't it been a fabulous day?' Rachel asked her new husband.

'Perfect. I'm not sure how either lot of parents really coped but at least they had their wish for a church ceremony and got to wear their posh hats.'

'But a beach party was exactly right for us.'

'It most certainly was. You looked gorgeous in your silky dress and with your hair loose. But then, you're a beautiful woman, Mrs Williams.'

'Married to a very handsome man.'

'Are you sure you're not disappointed to have come here for our honeymoon?'

'How could I be? It's the most beautiful country in the world. And this is one of the most beautiful places in that country.'

'Our parents would be shocked. They think we drove off to the airport.'

'Instead we drove just twenty miles from home. This is just such a perfect beach, isn't it?'

'Absolutely.'

'Can I have some more champagne, please?'

He poured her another glass and topped up his own.

'Here's to Cornwall. And here's to us,' he whispered.

'I love you,' she replied.

The End

We do hope that you have enjoyed reading this large print book.

Did you know that all of our titles are available for purchase?

We publish a wide range of high quality large print books including:
Romances, Mysteries, Classics
General Fiction
Non Fiction and Westerns

Special interest titles available in large print are:
The Little Oxford Dictionary
Music Book, Song Book
Hymn Book, Service Book

Also available from us courtesy of Oxford University Press:
Young Readers' Dictionary
(large print edition)
Young Readers' Thesaurus
(large print edition)

For further information or a free brochure, please contact us at:
Ulverscroft Large Print Books Ltd.,
The Green, Bradgate Road, Anstey,
Leicester, LE7 7FU, England.
Tel: (00 44) **0116 236 4325**
Fax: (00 44) **0116 234 0205**

When Kathleen Fitzgerald left Ireland twenty years ago, she never planned to return. In England she married firefighter Daniel Jackson and settled down to raise their family. However, when Dan is injured in the line of duty, events have a ripple effect, bringing challenges and new directions to the lives of Dan, Kathleen and their children, as well as Kathleen's parents and her brother, Stephen. How will the members of this extended family cope with their season of change?

CHERRY BLOSSOM LOVE

Maysie Greig

Beth was in love with her boss, but he could only dream of the brief passionate interlude he had shared with a Japanese girl long ago, and of the child he had never seen. Beth agrees to accompany him to Japan in search of his daughter. There perhaps, the ghost of Madame Butterfly would be laid, and he would turn to her for solace . . . Her loyal heart is lead along dark and dangerous paths before finding the love she craves.

THE SEABRIGHT SHADOWS

Valerie Holmes

Elizabeth, bound to a marriage she wants no part in, is strong willed and determined to free herself from the arrangement her father Silas has made. But she is trapped. The family's fortunes are linked to and dependent upon her marriage to Mr Timothy Granger, a man she despises. It takes a bold act of courage and the interference of her Aunt Jessica to make her see the future in a different light and save the family from ruin.

THE TWO OF US

Jennifer Ames

When Mark Dexter, visiting Australia, invited Janet to work in his publishing house in the United States, she thought he was offering her heaven. They had an adventurous and thrilling trip by plane to New York, lingering in Fiji and Havana; but when they reached New York Janet found she could not get away from Julian Gaden, an odd character whom Mark had introduced her to in a Sydney night club . . .